MAIL-ORDER BRIDES OF THE WEST:

DEBRA HOLLAND

ISBN: 978-1-939813-38-1

Published in the United States of America

Mail-Order Brides of the West Series

This book is dedicated to:

Louella Nelson,
Teacher, editor, and dearest friend.

You've been with me every step of the way on this writing journey, Lou.

It's due to you that my stories are so successful.
I couldn't have done it without you.

Acknowledgments

Many thanks go to:

Editors: Linda Carroll-Bradd, Adeli Britto

Formatter: Author E.M.S.

Cover Artists: Delle Jacobs, John Mitchell

Audiobook Narrator: Lara Asmundson

My family members:
Christine Holland, Niece and assistant
Mindy Codner Freed, Cousin and personal assistant
Honey Holland, Mom and sharp-eyed final reader

The members of Pioneer Hearts Facebook Group
For their love of historical Western romance, their support for
me as an author, giving me their opinions, looking up facts I
needed for this story, and most especially, their demands that
Prudence's have her own book.

Of my dear Pioneer Hearts Friends,
Special kudos go to Lisa Rumsey, super fan, who has posted on
her Facebook page almost every week (and lately daily)
how much she's been looking forward to Prudence.

Also to Samara Crider,
Who, when I needed last minute help for a guest blog the day
before this book was due, found an original 1896 recipe for
biscuits and supplied a photo from a batch she'd made.

I'm so very grateful to my readers!

MAIL-ORDER BRIDES OF THE WEST:

Prudence

1886

One week after
Mail-Order Brides of the West: Darcy

and seven years before
Wild Montana Sky

Chapter One

St. Louis, Missouri
1886

In the kitchen of the Mail-Order Brides of the West Agency, Prudence Crawford slid her tray of biscuits from the oven of the huge cast-iron stove. *This time my batch will be better than that fat cow's!* With the back of her wrist, she pushed a straggle of hair off her damp forehead, wishing she was reading in the shade of the garden, rather than slaving over a hot stove in the summer heat.

With nothing better to do than learn cooking and housekeeping, she'd begun a campaign to best the only other potential bride remaining at the agency. As far as Prudence was concerned, Bertha Bucholtz's skill in baking was her only redeeming quality. Her bread and rolls tasted heavenly and practically melted in your mouth.

So far Prudence had produced perfectly edible efforts, but her biscuits weren't as good as Bertha's. Today, determined to finally beat the other bride, she'd copied the woman's every move and used the exact same measurements.

As Prudence carried the tray to the counter, she inhaled the scent and eyed the biscuits, taking satisfaction in their light puffy shape and pale golden color.

Bertha hovered nearby, wringing her hands, an anxious expression in her wide-set blue eyes.

Usually the other bride was as placid as a bovine, but Prudence delighted in shattering the woman's serenity.

After picking up a hot pad, Bertha stepped to the stove and removed her tray. With obvious care to stay out of elbow range lest she end up with a jab to her well-padded ribs, she set her golden trophies next to Prudence's.

The cook Dona, a big, raw-boned woman with a no-nonsense air, leaned forward to examine the two trays. Using tongs, she scooped up one of Prudence's biscuits and one of Bertha's, placing them side-by-side on a plate.

Prudence studied the biscuits. To her eyes, they looked the same—puffy and golden—sure to taste delicious.

Dona broke one open. A lovely curl of steam wafted out. "We'll let them cool a minute." She jerked her chin at the big pot simmering on the stovetop. "Finish the soup, Miss Crawford, while Miss Bucholtz whips up the batter for a cake."

Although tempted to answer with a snide remark at the curt order, Prudence held her tongue. Her barbs didn't affect Dona, and a time or two, the cook had brandished a wooden spoon, threatening to hit her with the utensil.

Prudence had rushed to Mrs. Seymour, the owner of the agency, to complain about the cook's rude behavior. But the matron had only raised her eyebrows and calmly said to mind her manners lest Dona carry out her threat. Weeks later, the response still stung.

Resentfully, Prudence moved toward the stove to stir the soup, thinking she should add more onion, except she didn't want her eyes tearing and her hands stinking. Instead, she diced another carrot and tossed the pieces into the pot, inhaling the scent of garlic and oregano.

Minestrone. No matter how she tried, she never achieved soup as good as Lina Napolitano's. Although Prudence never admitted her preference to anyone, she loved the flavorful Italian soup Lina had concocted from a bit of this and a handful of that.

Just thinking of Lina heightened Prudence's resentment. The woman was happily matched to a man in that hick town of Sweetwater Springs in Montana Territory. The new Mrs. Barrett wrote ecstatic accounts of her life with her husband and young stepson, their farm, and her friendships with Trudy Flanigan and Darcy Walker—the other two mail-order brides who'd moved to Sweetwater Springs. Although Prudence would never choose a *farmer*, she envied Lina's happiness, as well as the good fortune of the other five mail-order brides who'd found love in Montana Territory.

Marriages, humph. She gave the soup an angry stir with a wooden spoon, splashing some over the side of the pot. The liquid hissed on the stovetop.

"Mind what you're doing, Miss Crawford," Dona said sharply, pointing a knife in Prudence's direction. "You can scrub the stove after we've finished the meal."

Prudence shot the cook a baleful glare.

The woman matched her look with one of firmness. "The biscuits have cooled enough."

Eager to see the outcome, Prudence abandoned the minestrone and moved toward the cook.

Dona broke the two rolls into threes. Handing them a piece from each, she said, "We'll start with Miss Bucholtz's, then sample Miss Crawford's."

Bertha slid over to the other side of the cook, smoothing her bib apron over her ample middle before accepting the two morsels.

Dona took a bite of Bertha's, chewing and swallowing. She gave the woman an approving nod. "Excellent, as always."

Nodding, Bertha beamed, her smile wide on her broad face.

The cook sampled Prudence's, her head slowly bobbing as she chewed and swallowed. "You've certainly come a long way with your biscuits, Miss Crawford." She waved toward

Prudence's tray. "You must take pride in your improvement. Any husband will be pleased by these."

Her stomach tightened. "But not as good as Bertha's?" Prudence asked, her voice rising in disbelief.

"Not quite."

Still not convinced, Prudence sampled Bertha's biscuit, and then took a bite of her own. The two tasted almost the same, although Bertha's was slightly mellower. Had she snuck in a smidge of buttermilk this time?

Once again, I'm not good enough. The sting of being second best made the bite stick in her craw. "We did everything the *same!*"

Dona's smile held pity. She gestured to the trays of biscuits. "Oh, no, my dear Miss Crawford. That isn't the case at all. For, you see, Miss Bucholtz adds an additional ingredient to the food she makes, the most special one of all—"

"She did *not.*" Prudence almost growled each word. "I watched everything Bertha did. *Matched* everything she did."

"But the missing ingredient isn't something you can see, Miss Crawford," the cook chided, wagging a finger at Prudence. "For Miss Bucholtz adds *love* into each batch of biscuits she bakes. You, unfortunately…well, yours are tainted with resentment, dislike, bitterness…."

Her face burning as if the cook had thrown scalding water over her, Prudence felt her frustration boil over. She grabbed her tray, uncaring that the metal was still hot enough to burn, and flung it across the kitchen. Biscuits flew through the air, and the tray clanged against the stove before clattering to the wood floor.

Mrs Seymour chose that moment to walk through the door. One edible projectile bounced off the skirt of her navy-blue dress. The matron stepped back to avoid more mayhem, then strode into the kitchen. "Prudence Crawford! Are you two years old to have such a tantrum?"

Far from quenching Prudence's ire, the harshness of the reprimand enflamed her. Angry heat burned through her chest into her face. She grabbed Bertha's tray and smashed it to the floor to join the other one.

Frowning, the matron surveyed the mess. "I have *never* witnessed such childish behavior from a grown woman."

"Someone's parents spared the rod too much," Dona muttered while shaking her head.

Mrs. Seymour flicked a reproving glance at the cook before her gaze bored into Prudence. "Pick up everything *immediately.* Take the ruined ones out to the pigs. That is, unless you want to save something for yourself, for you *certainly* won't be served luncheon after wasting food."

"I won't eat food from the floor," Prudence snapped, offended by the command.

"Very well. Go hungry, then. After you have fed the pigs, you and Bertha will join me in my office. There is a matter we must discuss."

The angry steam inside her deflated. Her head high, Prudence refused to let the three women see her embarrassment. *Yes, throwing the trays of biscuits was a bit much.* But she'd been so angry. *Adding love to the batter, indeed!*

Prudence lifted the bottom of the apron she wore over her blue day dress and formed a carryall. She stooped to grab a biscuit and tossed it into the apron. Her burned fingers hurt, but her pride wouldn't permit her to stop and run cold water over them.

Silently, Bertha bent down and gathered two, offering them to Prudence.

Resentment flared that the other woman had witnessed her humiliation. *How dare she be so helpful.* "Don't bother," she said tartly.

Bertha scuttled away, light on her feet despite her bulky body.

Still seething, Prudence picked up the remaining biscuits. When she'd recovered all of them, she marched outside and around the garden shed to the pigpen, where a sow and her litter resided.

She wrinkled her nose at the stench, picked a biscuit from the bunch in her apron, and flung it at the sow. The biscuit bounced off the pig's side with a dull thud. Liking the feeling, Prudence aimed each one at a pig, missing most of her shots.

The animals didn't seem to mind her attack. The sow turned to her in almost-human puzzlement before moving to grab the nearest biscuit.

The one-sided battle deflated Prudence's indignation. She released her apron and shook it out, hating having to wear the protective garment like a servant. Until arriving at the agency, Prudence had never donned one. The Crawfords had servants to do the menial tasks of cooking and housekeeping. But after the first kitchen disaster at the agency, she'd learned to shield her dresses or she would ruin them all, for she no longer had parents who'd replaced them.

Her shoulders slumped. The Crawfords had a comfortable lifestyle until her father grew senile, mismanaging his company. Her mother's preoccupation with taking care of her husband contributed to her own ill health and kept her from noticing the growing pile of unpaid bills. For all that she was good with calculations, Prudence never bothered with the boring business, tuning out her father whenever he'd tried discussing his affairs. *Fool that I was. I will never make that mistake again!*

When her parents died within months of each other, Prudence had to sell the St. Louis mansion and most of the family's possessions to pay off their debts. Unfortunately, her lack of beauty and wealth coupled with a reputation for being *difficult* precluded any local swain from wanting to court her. Her only choice was to leave the area and hope to marry a well-to-do man who didn't know about her history, which is why she'd chosen to become a mail-order bride. But six months had passed without the appearance of her future husband.

Prudence hated everything about living at the agency awaiting a match. *Where is he?* she demanded to the heavens. *Where is the wealthy man who will rescue me from menial chores and set me up in my proper sphere—a mansion stocked with servants?*

A quiet voice added, *where is the husband who will love me?*

Prudence thrust aside that preposterous thought. *Love doesn't matter.* Her parents had loved each other and look what happened to them. Only wealth and status were important.

Hopefully a handsome husband, as well—or at least one she could tolerate. An *attractive* rich husband would most definitely expect a pretty wife, something Prudence wasn't.

Dusting off her apron, she headed toward the house. After a few steps, she paused, admiring the big red Victorian with the three-story tower. The home she'd grown up in was far more elaborate, but the Seymour house managed to be both elegant and homey, and secretly she often pretended the place belonged to her.

Wanting to avoid the kitchen, Prudence entered through the glass doors of a small conservatory at the side of the garden. She moved through a paneled hallway to the front of the house, avoiding Juniper, the maid, who was polishing the frames of the paintings hanging on the wall.

The smell of lemon oil and beeswax followed Prudence through the double parlor where she paused at the open door of Mrs. Seymour's office overlooking the street. The octagonal room was her favorite in the house. Light flooded through the large windows, all of them draped with lace curtains.

Although she'd prefer to head toward a cushioned window seat, she saw Bertha already sitting in one of the two chairs in front of Mrs. Seymour's desk. Making sure her face was out of the matron's sight, Prudence flung the plump woman a snooty glance and flounced over to sit in the adjacent chair.

Bertha's chubby cheeks colored, and she glanced away.

Mrs. Seymour examined the two of them for a few minutes, her dark blue eyes sharp.

Not for the first time, Prudence thought how the older woman would still be attractive if she'd taken better care to shield her skin from the sun and coiffed her brown hair to minimize the white streak near her forehead.

The matron moved a stack of envelopes to the side of the desk. "I've decided to close the agency for a while and spend some time with Evie in Y Knot. My visit was far too short. I want to be with her and Chance during her pregnancy and the first months of the baby's life."

Close the agency? Dread tightened Prudence's stomach. *What will I do?*

Mrs. Seymour gave Bertha a sympathetic glance. "I'm so sorry that I've not found you a match. With no new suitable inquiries and those two men who seemed like good candidates finding brides elsewhere...." Shaking her head, she made a helpless gesture. "I simply can't understand why your match has taken so long."

Bertha looked down and crossed her arms over her billowing stomach. "I guess it's my shape," she mumbled.

"I don't think that's the case, my dear Bertha. Perhaps the good Lord has a very special man in mind for you, and we must be patient a while longer."

Prudence held back an unladylike snort.

Bertha slid a sideways glance at her before turning to Mrs. Seymour. "Been thinking that it's time to go home. There's nothing for me here. I've enjoyed learning from you and Dona. You've taught me a lot. I plan to hire out as a cook."

Mrs. Seymour let out a sigh. "You are certainly well suited for such a position, Bertha, and I will be happy to provide a reference. And since your home is close by, if the right match comes before I leave, I will notify you."

"Thank you." Bertha rose and nodded. Her expression crumpled as if she were about to cry. "I'll go pack." She hurried from the room.

Mrs. Seymour waited a moment then gave Prudence a sharp glance. "You realize that you've driven Bertha away with your nasty behavior? She didn't have to leave the agency just yet."

Prudence shrugged. She didn't care what happened to the cow.

"I blame myself for not keeping a tighter rein on you. Evie's situation—her running away, my visit to her, her pregnancy—has distracted me." The matron shook her head and sighed. "The man who takes you on will certainly have his hands full. I pity him."

Nonsense! "I'll not act this way with a husband." *I'll have no need to.*

The matron's eyebrows rose. "And how will you stop yourself? Controlling one's temper, one's poor impulses, takes *self-discipline*, Prudence. A trait I've never seen you exercise. The first time you feel hurt or angry with the poor man, cutting words will fly out of your mouth, and you'll probably throw something at him."

Never!

"I advise you to reflect upon things you are grateful for as a way to learn to keep a more amiable attitude. For if you don't learn self-restraint, you will jeopardize your marriage, making both of you miserable. Honey catches far more flies than vinegar—a truth that applies men, too."

A quiver of fear went through her. Prudence shoved the feeling away, not really believing the woman. *Why wouldn't I be kind to my own husband?* But still, she made a mental note to be careful to control her temper.

"Not to mention that men can be..." Mrs. Seymour hesitated, brushing imaginary dust off the surface of the desk. "*Rougher* in their reactions, especially if they've been imbibing alcohol. Goodness knows, I've wanted to smack you sometimes. But a husband might actually do so, with all the power of the law behind him."

Prudence gripped the armrests of the chair. "He wouldn't dare!"

"I'm afraid I've seen such behavior far too many times."

"Well, that won't happen to *me*."

Mrs. Seymour threw up her hands. "You are too stubborn for your own good. The consequences of your behavior will be on your own head." She lowered her hands to the desk, stood, and leaned forward. "You have until the end of the month to find a match, Prudence. *Eleven days.* Then, regardless, I'm leaving for Y Knot, and you must find somewhere else to live. Had you been a more amiable bride, I would have postponed my plans until I could match you. But today was the last straw. I no longer feel any sense of obligation toward you."

Prudence stared at Mrs. Seymour in shock. "But I don't have

anywhere else to go," she blurted, and then could have cut off her tongue for admitting such a vulnerability.

With a wave of her hand, Mrs. Seymour dismissed Prudence's words. "I'm afraid that's not my concern. You have made your bed, Prudence Crawford, and now you must lie in it."

Chapter Two

Morgan's Crossing, Montana Territory

Friday morning Michael Morgan, the self-appointed mayor of Morgan's Crossing, Montana Territory, stood on the porch of his newly built home and savored a cup of coffee. With an air of smug satisfaction, he surveyed his domain. The August sunshine washed the area with bright light, harshly illuminating the rough clapboard or log buildings of the town. He soaked in heat like a lizard, storing the warmth—a memory to take out during the dark, cold winter.

To the right, the dirt road leading to his gold mine bent around a hill. From Michael's viewpoint, he couldn't see the company office, the blacksmith shop, or the building housing his guards. To the left lay the town—every square inch owned by him, with all fifty-one of the inhabitants firmly under his thumb.

Next came Rigsby's Saloon—named for the bartender—the barracks where his miners roomed, the company store, and some individual houses—seven in all—where his workers who had families lived, as well as one rented by the teamster and Michael's former cabin, which was currently empty. Last was the whitewashed combination meeting house, church, schoolhouse—

not that the building was used for school. With only ten children in the town—half barely knee-high—he saw no need to hire a teacher. Only occasionally was the building actually used for Catholic mass, whenever Father Fredrick made his rounds, once every month or so.

Even more rarely did Reverend Norton undertake the two-day journey from Sweetwater Springs to hold a Protestant service. Most Sundays, he was too busy seeing to the needs of his own parish. Not that Michael minded the absence of either man of God. Occasional church attendance suited him fine, but he preferred to work on Sundays in the quiet hours when folks tended to keep to themselves.

He took a sip of his coffee, conscious of a feeling of anticipation that lifted his spirits from the sense of tedium he'd settled into lately. Now that his house was built—complete with three bedrooms, a parlor, an office, and a kitchen—he was ready to take the next step in his plan. *A wife.* He needed a Mrs. Morgan to warm his bed, do his laundry, cook his meals, keep the place clean, and provide him with a son or two to carry on the business.

He imagined strolling down the dirt road of Morgan's Crossing with a beautiful woman on his arm, the envy of all the townsfolk. *Oh, yes, I'm most definitely in need of a wife.*

The only problem was the lack of any available women in Morgan's Crossing and only a precious few in Sweetwater Springs. Even if a suitable lady living in the bigger town caught his eye, he didn't have the time or inclination to spend the four-day, round-trip journey, riding back and forth to court her.

No, Michael had a far more expedient plan. He was sending for a mail-order bride from a reputable agency—one that had already provided several wives for the men of Sweetwater Springs.

Motion on the dirt street caught his eye.

Portia Rossmore, heavy with child, waddled past.

Not for the first time, Michael pondered the travesty of the delicate, blonde beauty married to the abusive oaf Clyde

Rossmore. He supposed his foreman was handsome enough in a brutish way and capable of acting personably—at least until someone crossed him. He'd most likely hidden his drinking while he courted her. "Good morning, Portia," Michael called.

She barely turned her head, lifting her hand in a slight wave before looking straight ahead.

Even the quick glimpse of her face, framed by a faded blue sunbonnet, was enough for him to see her black eye. Michael growled, restraining himself from rushing after her, demanding to know what had happened. He knew from experience Portia would only deny Clyde had hit her. Nothing stopped the man from beating on his wife—the fairest creature in Morgan's Crossing.

Michael had tried to stop the miner, using threats, bribes, and even, one time, his fists. But each attempt only enraged Clyde, and Portia paid the price, leaving Michael feeling remorseful. The only other thing he could do was fire the man, or, at least, threaten to do so. But he never made threats he wasn't willing to follow through with, and he couldn't bear to think of what would happen to the woman if her husband lost his job. Clyde would probably beat her to death, causing Michael to feel responsible.

He hadn't given up on finding ways to limit the man's abuse, but so far he'd had no new solutions.

I could kill Clyde. Michael had pondered the idea before coming to the conclusion that murdering the brute would only cause trouble for himself, and he'd lose his best worker. *Too bad some other man doesn't steal Portia away, taking her far from Clyde's reach.*

But that man wasn't Michael. Even if he loved Portia—which he didn't—and was willing to bestir himself on her behalf, he desired a wife with more spirit— one who'd threaten him with a frying pan if he ever tried to hit her.

Michael laughed at the image he'd conjured up and took a sip of his coffee. *As if I'd ever stoop so low as to hurt a woman.*

He turned and walked through the double doors of the vestibule, past a second set with glass panels that opened into the entryway of the house. Inside, windows let in plenty of light, highlighting walnut woodwork and plain walls in need of wallpaper. Someday, he'd replace a few of the windows with stained glass.

His study was on one side of the entry, the parlor on the other, empty except for a new settee and his comfortable chair, the leather worn and cracking in places.

Walking into his office, Michael sensed the empty bookshelves mocking him. Even in the winter, he had no time to read. He was usually too busy struggling with the accounting for his various businesses. In his spare time, he read the newspaper.

I'll fill the shelves eventually. Books will be part of the decor. Or perhaps his bride would bring books with her, like he'd heard Trudy Flanigan had. Sweetwater Springs was a hotbed of gossip about the three women who'd arrived as mail-order brides. He'd gotten an earful on his last visit to the town. Michael hadn't yet clapped eyes on any of the brides, but when he'd hefted a glass in Hardy's Saloon on his last trip, he'd paid attention as the men described each woman quite thoroughly, singing their praises.

In addition, he received updates from El Davis, the teamster who made the run from the railroad stop in Sweetwater Springs to Morgan's Crossing every couple of weeks. The man brought gossip along with the goods and supplies loaded in his wagon.

On Michael's desk lay a folded newspaper. He'd ordered a subscription to the *Billings Herald* after he heard the periodical contained the advertisement for the Mail-Order Brides of the West Agency.

Setting down his coffee mug, he took a seat at the desk, picked up the newspaper already folded to the page he wanted, and reread the ad he'd studied several times.

MAIL-ORDER BRIDES OF THE WEST AGENCY
SEEKS BACHELORS OF GOOD REPUTATION
FOR QUALITY BRIDES PROFICIENT IN
COOKING AND HOUSEKEEPING
Must own a house and be able to provide for a wife.
References required, preferably from your minister or other
reputable person who is familiar with your character.

**In your response, state details about your appearance,
location, level of education, vocation, and home,
as well as what you require in a wife.
$50.00 includes agency fee and train ticket.**

The ad went on to give details about where to apply for a bride. From the top drawer, he withdrew a piece of stationary and set the paper on the top of the desk. He picked up his pen, dipped the tip in the inkwell, and began to write the owner of the agency.

Dear Mrs. Seymour,

I'm Michael Morgan, the mayor of Morgan's Crossing, Montana Territory, a town two days' ride from Sweetwater Springs, which is also the nearest railway stop. I am thirty-five years old and well educated. Not to display vanity, but to provide information to a potential bride, I've been told on more than one occasion that I'm a fine figure of a man, possessing a handsome countenance with all my hair and teeth.

Michael paused, wondering if he should lie about knowing the other mail-order brides, but then figured since he was riding into the town, he'd meet them, so the statement wouldn't be a lie.

I'm acquainted with the women you've sent to Sweetwater Springs—all worthy wives, who (from all accounts) have made their husbands quite content.

I am the owner of a gold mine.

No need to add that the miners had so far extracted barely enough gold to pay the costs of running the mine.

In addition, I own the businesses and other buildings in Morgan's Crossing.

Best not mention the saloon.

I have recently finished building the largest house in town—a veritable mansion, which could use a discerning woman's touch.

A mansion only in comparison to the other houses.

I have furnished my home with well-crafted pieces of the latest design.

At least the bed, the settee, and my desk are.

But I have plenty of space left for a wife to decorate to her heart's content.

15

As long as the furnishings don't cost too much.

I require a wife between the ages of twenty and twenty-seven who's refined and elegant—a suitable first lady for Morgan's Crossing.

Michael remembered his earlier thoughts of Portia.

I'd appreciate a woman of inner strength and spirit.

I've enclosed your fee and look forward to the arrival of my bride.

Sincerely,

Michael Morgan

He reread the letter, thinking about the risk he was taking in selecting a lifetime companion sight unseen. But he had no choice, for suitable alternatives didn't exist. Satisfied with the missive, he rose and walked over to the safe, hidden behind the lake scene painted by one of his sisters that hung on the wall.

Michael took down the picture, pulled the key from his pocket, unlocked the metal door, and swung it open. Inside laid a stack of bills, a leather bag containing gold nuggets, and a Mason jar half full of gold dust.

He scooped up $50 worth using a $10 measuring spoon he'd designed, trickling the gold dust into the envelope. When he reached the correct amount, he added another $5 for good measure, just in case the woman lost some when she opened the letter. He licked the edge of the flap, grimacing at the taste, pressed it shut, and set the bulky envelope on his desk. Later, he would seal the point with wax.

The bell next to the outer doors clanged. Probably Mrs. Tisdale with his meal.

His stomach rumbled in response. Until now, Michael hadn't realized he was hungry. He preferred to have the woman cook at her house and bring him the meals rather than having her underfoot in his kitchen. He paid for the extra food, which she shared with her family, so her son and grandchild, an appealing boy, ate far better than they would have on a miner's wages.

Locking the safe, he replaced the painting, and then left the office to answer the door. "Good afternoon, Mrs. Tisdale."

"Afternoon, Mr. Morgan." She gave him a gap-toothed grin and handed over a tin plate covered by a second one. "I have ham, eggs, and biscuits for you. Still piping hot, they are."

With gruff thanks, Michael accepted the plate from her and walked back into the house. He set the plate on his desk, for he had no dining or kitchen table yet, and stared at the envelope that would change his future.

I could end up with an ugly shrew. The thought made his belly cramp and banished his hunger.

Acquiring a wife is essential. He took a deep breath and reviewed his decision.

Before he mailed the letter, Michael planned to see the three mail-order brides in Sweetwater Springs to ascertain if the women were all the gossip had proclaimed them to be. Hopefully, they could suggest a wife from among the women they'd known at the agency. Only after he saw and spoke with them would he make a final decision.

His stomach tightened. *A final, irrevocable decision.*

On the journey to Sweetwater Springs, Michael hadn't made as good time as he'd expected, due to his black gelding King picking up a stone in his hoof. In a foul mood, he arrived at the town on Sunday, just about the time the service was ending, for he could see people spilling out from the church onto the dirt street. *I've come all this way, so I'd better not have lost the opportunity to view the brides before sending off my letter.*

Outside Hardy's, he saw Slim, a cowboy who frequented the saloon. Michael reined in next to the man. "I understand three women are newly arrived to Sweetwater Springs. Mail-order brides. Are any of them still here?"

The man smirked. "You're in luck. All three are in town with their husbands." His grin widened, showing missing teeth. He pointed to the front of the church to a trio of men and women conversing.

Michael recognized Jonah Barrett and Seth Flanigan from meeting them at Hardy's Saloon a time or two. Barrett held a toddler, who must be his half-breed son. He could see the bonds of friendship between the three couples, obvious by how close they stood, their conversation, and their laughter.

Now that he had a chance to fulfill his errand, Michael relaxed and his bad mood eased. A longing to be part of a couple and one of a tight-knit group of friends seized him.

Jonah Barrett jerked a thumb in the direction of the livery, and the men ambled away, probably to fetch their wagons.

The women remained in a tight cluster, their friendship apparent in how they bent their heads to each other, the frequent smiles and touches on the arm. They all wore broad-brimmed straw hats with flowers and pale summery dresses.

I want that kind of warmth from a wife. Michael rode closer to better see them, halting King a few feet away.

The brides broke off their discussion and turned to face him.

Michael eyed each woman up and down, taking stock of their faces and bodies. None was the perfect woman he'd wished for in a wife, but all were more than passable. The blond-haired, blue-eyed one was the prettiest. From how he'd heard her described, he figured she was Trudy Flanigan.

He admired the lush curves of the Italian-looking one, who must be Lina Barrett. The Barretts had the farm off a road leading to Morgan's Crossing.

Next to her was a tall, plain woman who possessed intelligent gray eyes and an air of elegance. She wore an expensive silvery gown. *Must be Darcy Walker—the rich woman who'd married a recluse, the man he hadn't recognized from the group.*

Michael imagined if he combined all three, he'd have the perfect wife, but he'd be content with any one of them. Reassured, he decided to go ahead with sending the letter to the bridal agency.

Mrs. Walker raised her eyebrows in haughty inquiry.

Not at all deterred, he tipped his hat to the trio. "I'm Michael Morgan of Morgan's Crossing. I'm sure you've heard of me," he said with certainty. "I'm the mine owner. Own the whole town, for that matter."

Mrs. Walker's chin lifted the slightest bit. "Why no, I haven't."

"I've heard of you mail-order brides, and I wanted to see for myself what kind of women you are."

"Why ever would you care?" Mrs. Walker's tone was as cool as her eyes.

He leaned a forearm on the saddle horn. "I want a bride for myself. But not just any woman will do. After all, I have my standards."

The Italian one chuckled and exchanged silent glances with the other two.

"And what are you looking for in a wife, Mr. Morgan?" Mrs. Flanigan asked sweetly.

"Well, the ad says you women are already well-trained in cooking and housekeeping...."

"That is correct." Lina Barrett said.

Mrs. Barrett's Italian accent was too prominent for his taste. "I require a woman of *elegance*," Michael told them. "My prospective wife must be educated and well-bred—a suitable first lady of Morgan's Crossing and a fine helpmate to me. The kind of woman who is simply *not* to be found anywhere around here, so I must send away for her."

"A first lady for Morgan's Crossing..." Mrs. Flanigan drew out the words as if thinking. "I do believe there might be someone at the agency who'd suit you perfectly." Her blue eyes sparkled. With a smile, she flicked a glance at the other two.

Mrs. Barrett's firm nod of agreement made corkscrew tendrils of dark hair bounce around her face.

"Be sure to write and ask for Prudence Crawford." Mrs. Walker's words were crisp. "Miss Crawford comes from a prominent St. Louis family. I believe you'll find her to be *exactly* the wife you need."

Prudence Crawford. Michael made a mental note of the name.

"Oh, but Prudence would never go to that pokey little town."

Mrs. Flanigan waved her hand in an airy dismissal. "Our *dear* Prudence deserves a nice house in a place where she can be a leader of society."

Mrs. Barrett's brown eyes danced. She bit her lip and remained quiet.

Ruffled by having his town dismissed, Michael drew himself upright. "Miss Crawford will have that with me, ladies, I can assure you." He placed a hand on his chest to convey his sincerity. "I am the mayor of the town."

"So you said." Mrs. Walker waved her hand in dismissal. "Well then, Mr. Morgan, we wish you well in your choice of bride. Now—" She linked arms with her friends. "If you'll excuse us, we must join our husbands."

Michael nodded a regal farewell and urged King toward the train station, so lost in thought he barely acknowledged those he rode by. He didn't want to open the letter to add the specific request for Prudence Crawford and risk having the gold dust fall out. Nor did he have a second envelope to which he could transfer the letter and the gold dust. *I'll just have to write on the back.*

He pondered what to add. *In a recent conversation, (after I'd sealed this missive) Mrs. Walker, Mrs. Barrett, and Mrs. Flanigan urged me to request the hand of Miss Prudence Crawford in marriage.*

Chapter Three

Once Mr. Morgan's back was to them and he'd ridden out of earshot, Darcy Walker pulled her two companions to a stop. The three women looked at each other and burst into simultaneous laughter.

Darcy inhaled Lina's scent of roses and oregano and Trudy's lavender perfume and sent up a small prayer of gratitude for the friendship of these dear women.

Lina covered her mouth with her hand to stifle her boisterous laugh.

Trudy wiped a finger under her eyes. "Oh, dear. We are *so* wicked."

"We are indeed," Darcy cheerfully agreed. "And I'm not the least bit repentant. Pride goeth before a fall, as the good book says. And those two are in for quite a fall. Michael Morgan and Prudence Crawford deserve each other."

Frowning, Lina lowered her hand. "What if we've misjudged him? We'll have saddled him with a shrew, and he'll be miserable. We'll be to blame for his misery. And, *Madonna Mia,* what if they have a child? Can you imagine Prudence as a *mother?*"

Stricken, they stared at each other.

Darcy was the first to recover and patted Lina's shoulder. "I don't believe we've misjudged Mr. Morgan. We all have good instincts, and we each had the same reaction to the man." She made her tone teasing. "Just in case, I'll mail him my copy of *The Taming of the Shrew*, which he can use as an instruction manual."

Trudy tilted her head in the direction of the livery, a silent signal for them to continue walking. "I have a copy in the boxes of books I brought. I don't remember seeing it, so the book is probably still in the barn. When I find the volume, I'll replace your book, Darcy. One reading of that play was enough for me."

The women fell into step.

Lina chuckled. "Mrs. Seymour will be so grateful to have Prudence off her hands."

As a sudden unpleasant realization struck her, Darcy halted. "Oh, dear Lord," she exclaimed in dismay. "Ladies, do you realize what we've just done to ourselves?"

The other two stopped. After sharing a puzzled glance, they shook their heads.

"Instead of the whole West to choose from—where we'd never have to see or hear from her again—now, we'll have Prudence Crawford on our doorstep."

Lina released a theatrical groan. "Oh, no!"

Trudy fluttered her hands in a helpless gesture. "Well, you did say pride goeth before a fall, Darcy. Now we are repaid for our prideful efforts."

Trudy's right, Darcy thought with an uncomfortable clench of her stomach. *We were wrong to meddle.* "Morgan's Crossing is two days away." She tried to assure herself and her friends, even as dread weighed on her conscience. "While I'm sorry for the inhabitants of that town, I doubt we'll ever have to deal with Prudence Crawford Morgan. She certainly won't seek *us* out."

Lina's decisive nod set her black curls bouncing around her face. "That is *if* she even accepts Mr. Morgan. Don't forget, she's rejected other matches."

Trudy perked up. "That's true."

"You're right," Darcy agreed. "Lina, remember all the disparaging things Prudence said about Montana Territory when

Trudy and Evie first moved out here? And she was even more vocal with her opinion after you and Heather left."

"She won't accept Mr. Morgan. He has too many black marks against him." Trudy ticked off the points on her fingers. "Montana Territory. Small town. Near us."

Breathing out a sigh of obvious relief, Lina placed a hand to her chest. "Thank goodness. If she said one nasty thing about my little Adam, I'd box her ears, and Sheriff Rand would probably throw me in jail."

"Not if he knew Prudence," Darcy said in a wry tone. "He'd probably give you a medal."

Again, the three burst into laughter.

"I think we are safe." Darcy lifted her chin in the direction of the livery stable and slipped her hands around her friends' arms, marveling how they'd become so close in a few short months. "Come along, my dear mail-order brides. Our husbands await."

The mail's arrived. Prudence picked up the envelopes on the silver tray near the front door and flipped through them. She searched the return addresses, hoping for solicitations from potential husbands, for Mrs. Seymour's deadline was ticking away.

The first letter was from a woman she didn't recognize, the next from Evie Holcomb. She wrinkled her nose at the name, resenting how the servant girl had secretly taken the letter written by Chance Holcomb and run away to join him, depriving a *real* bridal candidate of a match.

Not that I'd have chosen a rancher. Prudence had no desire to live among cows. But she thought Evie didn't deserve happiness after such an egregious act. Unfairly, however, the maid had found love.

The third envelope was also from Y Knot. Although mail-order bride Kathryn Ford had taken several weeks to marry her farmer, Tobit Preece, she still managed to reel him in. Just the thought of another blissful marriage when she was still stuck at the agency annoyed Prudence.

But even living at the agency was better than living in a boarding house. Although Mrs. Seymour required Prudence to pay for a room of her own, the cost wasn't high because the bridal candidates performed the household tasks under the guise of "training to be wives." Living in a nice hotel would quickly use up her remaining funds, and the thought of a rooming somewhere cheap and shabby made her cringe.

The address on the fourth envelope was written in a strong masculine hand, and her heart gave a leap of hope. *Michael Morgan.* She liked that name—the alliteration, the rhythm.

But when Prudence saw the address, she felt her optimism seeping away. *Montana Territory*—the last area in the entire union where she'd consider moving. In addition to being a cold, out-of-the-way place, too many of the former mail-order brides lived there. She didn't want to be anywhere near those women. She looked closer at the return address. *Morgan's Crossing, not Sweetwater Springs or Y Knot.*

Something made Prudence turn over the envelope, and she saw a sentence scrawled across the back. Her name leaped out. Heart pounding, she read every word. Twice. Three times.

A man is asking for me! She wanted to shriek, to whirl in delight, but she restrained herself and reread the sentence, realizing that a recommendation from Trudy, Lina, and Darcy might not be a good thing. And if the man lived near enough to know her fellow brides, then that was too close for her liking. *Why would they recommend me?*

Still, Prudence was curious and carried the letters to Mrs. Seymour, who worked at her desk in the office. Without being asked, she took a seat, setting the other envelopes on the desk and handing the special one to the matron. "There's a letter from a suitor. Montana Territory."

The woman looked up. "Oh, then one of our brides must have referred him."

"He's asking for *me*." Prudence couldn't keep the glee from her tone.

Brows raised in puzzlement, Mrs. Seymour studied the address before turning over the envelope and reading the back. "You're right. This gentleman has requested you." The matron's expression made no secret of her surprise.

The woman's disbelief immediately caused Michael Morgan to seem more appealing. Prudence clasped her hands tight.

Mrs. Seymour took a letter opener and slit the top of the envelope. She pulled out the letter, and a shower of gold particles dusted the surface of the desk. "Goodness gracious!"

Prudence leaned forward to see better. "What is that?"

"Gold dust." She shook her head. "Whatever was the man thinking? I could have scattered this all over the carpeting and lost most of it. Run and get a bowl from the kitchen."

Prudence rose and hurried out. But instead of going all the way to the kitchen, she grabbed a cut-glass bowl of dried flowers from a nearby side table and upended it, scattering faded petals over the marble surface, and sending the faint scent of roses into the air. *Juniper can clean the mess later.*

Back in the office, she thrust the bowl at Mrs. Seymour and plopped into the chair.

The matron must have been just as curious for she didn't reprimand Prudence for not following orders. She gently shook the paper, sending glittering grains into the bowl. Then Mrs. Seymour carefully brushed the edge of the paper across the desk, sweeping the gold into the bowl. Once apparently satisfied that she'd caught every last flake, she unfolded the paper and began to read.

Prudence fidgeted with impatience, barely restraining herself from grabbing the letter from Mrs. Seymour to see the message from Mr. Morgan.

With an impassive expression, the matron handed over the paper.

Prudence skimmed the words, and with each sentence her excitement grew. She ended the letter and carefully reread what Michael had written. "He sounds perfect for me!"

"I agree that he does, although why the man would send me gold dust...."

"Probably to provide proof of his claim to own a mine," Prudence said with assurance. "Else we might not have believed him."

"You're right." Mrs. Seymour made a helpless wave of her hand, an uncommon gesture for the self-possessed matron. "But I'm not sure about his character. He hasn't enclosed references. We should write to Trudy for word of his character. She's lived in the area the longest."

"No need." Prudence scooted to the edge of the chair. "I'm satisfied with what he's stated about himself. Besides, the month is almost over, and you're anxious to start your journey to Y Knot."

"That's true," Mrs. Seymour said with unusual hesitation. "I'm reassured that you'll be near women I trust. I think if you make your peace with them, they'll forgive your past behaviors and assist you in adjusting to your new life."

Prudence shrugged, not at all concerned with trivial female friendships, especially with three whom she disliked. *They live too near. The only fly in the ointment. Well, that and the cold climate.*

"Do not dismiss the idea," Mrs. Seymour said sharply. "You'll find relationships with other women bring true comfort and support, something we are in dire need of at times."

Prudence, dazzled by the idea of being the first lady of Morgan's Crossing, didn't even want her fellow brides to know she was on her way to Montana Territory. She'd be happy if she never saw them again.

Although...perhaps at some point, she'd condescend to pay them a visit. *But I'll do so on my own terms.*

Prudence rose, clutching her precious letter. "If you'll excuse me, I must write Mr. Morgan immediately. There's no time to lose." Dazzled with excitement, she hurried from the room, rushing through the parlor and upstairs to her bedroom. After shutting the door behind her, she waltzed across the space between the four-poster bed and the wardrobe.

She patted a barrel in passing that held her grandmother's dishes, silverware, and serving pieces. "Soon you'll be in use again." Since her grandmother had willed them to her several years ago, the creditors couldn't demand they be sold to pay her father's debts like the rest of the contents of her family's home. Prudence imagined presiding over an elegant dining table, set with these pieces, the silver glittering in the candle and gaslight.

Four trunks holding her possessions were stacked on both sides of a dressing table, leaving only a small space for her to move around the bed. She could hardly wait to have her own home and unpack her belongings.

Prudence allowed herself one last twirl before taking a seat at the dressing table, which she used as a desk. She removed a piece of stationery from a box painted with flowers. She surveyed the calligraphied initials at the top, thinking how she'd have to order new stationery after the wedding. *Mrs. Michael Morgan. Prudence Morgan. Quite a distinctive name.*

Perhaps I should order the stationery and calling cards before I leave St. Louis. Hopefully, there's time, and if not, I'll have them shipped to Morgan's Crossing. Pleased with the idea, she reached for her pen, dipped the tip in the inkwell, and began to write.

My dear Mr. Morgan,

I take up my pen to write an acceptance of your proposal. She paused to calculate how long before she'd arrive in Sweetwater Springs. With six brides having already left for Montana Territory, even if Evie did sneak away, Prudence was all too familiar with the train schedule for a journey to that area.

I'll arrive in Sweetwater Springs on August 28th.

I look forward to becoming your wife and the first lady of Morgan's Crossing. After writing the words, Prudence paused and let out a happy sigh, imagining lording over everyone in the town.

Sincerely,

Prudence Crawford

Smiling, she signed her name with a flourish.

This will be the last time I write this signature. Soon I'll be Mrs. Michael Morgan.

She glanced up at herself in the oval mirror hanging over the dressing table, and her good feelings deflated, for no beauty was staring back at her. Her face was too thin and bony, her chin pointed, her hair dark and severe, and her eyes a pale blue that changed color depending on the hue of the dress she wore. She looked best in blues, greens, and purples.

For a moment her mind flashed back to her older sister, who'd died twelve years earlier. Familiar sadness made her chest tight. Lissa, the treasured beauty of the family, had been much older. Where Prudence's face was thin and bony, Lissa's was oval, her hair mink-brown. Their pale eyes were the same, but her sister had thick dark lashes and pretty pink lips. She was as sweet as she was pretty, and everyone adored her, including Prudence. Her sister's love made up for their parents' indifference to their plain younger daughter.

The Crawford home had been filled with Lissa's friends and suitors. Laughter and conversations and singing and the sound of the piano rang throughout the house. Prudence had often watched the festivities from a secret spot on the upstairs landing, counting the years until she'd be old enough to join the fun. Then Lissa died, and thereafter, silence shrouded their home.

And I became invisible.

Prudence tossed her head, as if shaking off an old memory, and pressed her lips together. *As first lady of Morgan's Crossing, I'll never be invisible again.*

Chapter Four

If I see one more piddling town, I'll scream. Prudence peered out of the grimy train window, the pressure in her chest growing heavier the closer they came to Sweetwater Springs. In Saint Louis, the windows had started out clear, but a summer shower in one area, followed by a dust storm in another, had obscured some of the view.

Prudence brushed some ashes off the rumbled gray linen traveling coat she wore to protect her dress. She hadn't anticipated meeting her fiancé in a disheveled state. Although she'd washed her hands and face at the last stop, she could do nothing to erase the smell of smoke permeating her clothing. After today's heat, she was desperately in need of a bath.

At some point, she'd fallen asleep with her head against the wall of the train, squishing her straw hat and breaking off one of the flowers. Another drooped over the brim, and she pushed the bloom back into place.

All Prudence had to offer Michael Morgan was her elegance, and now he'd take one look at her appearance and think he'd bought a pig in a poke. The weight on her chest grew heavier. Her mother's words came to her.

You can always tell a lady by her air of good breeding—how she carries herself, the grace in her every gesture. Despite Mother's obvious best effort at self-control, her well-modulated voice had held a sharp note, and Prudence felt gratified to have overset her mother's reserve, briefly capturing the attention she longed for.

Now she clutched the words of wisdom, straightening her shoulders and lifting her chin. She hoped to impress Michael Morgan with her *air*, so he wouldn't notice her plainness or the grimy state of her attire. *Or how I smell.*

The portly conductor strolled through the car, stopping in front of her seat. "Sweetwater Springs, Miss."

She nodded and thanked him. Normally, Prudence didn't pay attention to service people, but on this trip, she'd felt out of her element, and the man had treated her with kindness.

After pulling a lace-edged handkerchief from the cuff of her sleeve, she rubbed the cloth over her face, hoping she hadn't missed any smudges. *I should have packed my hand mirror in my satchel instead of the trunk.*

The train chugged into Sweetwater Springs. Prudence turned her head to view her destination, hoping for an improvement from the other towns she'd seen recently. The movement made the daisy on her hat flop over the brim. She pushed the limp flower into place, wondering if she should leave it be or snap off the stem.

Prudence had no eye for the buildings, instead focusing on the man in a black suit standing on the platform holding a pocket watch in his hand.

Surely that's him. Nervousness churned in her stomach.

He tucked the gold watch into his vest pocket and glanced at the train. He was handsome, with wide-set brown eyes, even features, and a strong chin. She liked that he was clean-shaven.

Pleasure and relief eased the pressure on Prudence's chest, and a bond of attraction seized her heart. *I can't believe he's mine!*

Michael had stopped by the parsonage before arriving at the train station. The Nortons invited him into their home to wash up and change into his best suit. The couple showed obvious excitement at the thought of welcoming another mail-order bride, even if she wouldn't be living in Sweetwater Springs. Their approval of his decision bolstered his spirits and dampened his doubts.

He'd paced back and forth across the platform of the train station, stopping every few minutes to check his gold pocket watch, even though he knew the train should be on time. With the mild late-summer weather, no reason existed for delay. But still the minutes seemed to stretch while he awaited his bride, anticipation and dread in equal measure swirling in his stomach.

Finally the engine came into view, churning up the track. With a screech and whoosh of brakes, the train slowed to a stop. *Right on time.* Michael stowed the watch in his vest pocket. Impatience tightened his muscles, and he tried to see through the dusty windows to spot his bride.

A portly conductor stepped out, holding a valise. He reached up to help a woman off the train whose gray traveling coat shrouded her slender figure.

Is she the one?

Her head was down, watching her step. The brim of a straw hat hid her face from view.

At least she isn't fat.

No other woman exited the train, so Michael knew this must indeed be Prudence Crawford. Like a hammer on stone, his heart knocked against his ribs. Tap, tap, tap. He moved toward her, aware of his whole future resting on this moment.

Once Miss Crawford stepped onto the platform, she released the conductor's hand and thanked him before looking at Michael, surveying him with pale gray eyes.

Disappointment stabbed him. Her narrow, plain face, sharp chin, and uninteresting eyes were not what he'd expected. Her wan smile failed to bring beauty to her features.

I've made a mistake! It took everything in him to hold his ground and not turn tail and run. He'd given his word to marry this woman, and Michael Morgan didn't renege on his promises.

He stepped forward, bowed, and took her hand. "My dear Miss Crawford. Welcome to Sweetwater Springs." He brought her hand to his lips, and then released her to reach for her valise.

The conductor gave Michael the satchel.

"Thank you." He turned back to his bride. "I'm so glad you're here. Reverend and Mrs. Norton await us. You'll be able to freshen up before the wedding." His throat tightened, cutting off any further attempt to speak. Since Michael couldn't force out another false statement, he tried to manage a false smile, hoping he was a better actor than he felt.

The baggage handlers unloaded four trunks and a wooden barrel.

He nodded in their direction. "I have men to load your luggage in wagon and drive everything to the parsonage. But I thought you'd appreciate a stroll through town. Stretch your legs...uh." Michael belatedly remembered he shouldn't have mentioned *legs* to a lady. "Stretch your *limbs* after sitting so long."

She nodded but didn't speak.

He wondered what her voice sounded like. "You can wash up and change at the parsonage before the wedding ceremony...." Realizing he was repeating himself, he stuttered to a stop and mutely extended his elbow to her.

After a quick upward glance at him, she lowered her eyelids. Her long pale brown lashes hid the expression in her eyes.

With a stab of guilt, he wondered if Miss Crawford could tell his...not revulsion, exactly. *Reluctance* was a better description.

Chapter Five

The initial dismay in Michael Morgan's eyes at the first sight of Prudence, knifed her heart. He'd quickly veiled his expression, but the damage was done.

Prudence fisted her hand to keep from pressing a palm against her chest to contain the pain. *I mustn't let him see my hurt.* She mustered up a smile, moving forward by rote.

His formal greeting echoed in her mind, and doubts seized her. Prudence had all she could do to hold her facial muscles in a serene expression—or the closest she could come to one. *Should I go forward with this marriage?*

Moving like an automaton, Prudence had taken his arm, allowing him to escort her down the wooden steps and into the dirt street. She only vaguely registered the buildings, a brick mercantile, false-fronted wooden structures, a white-steepled church. After all, this wasn't her town. *Surely Morgan's Crossing will be a more illustrious place?*

But after seeing all the other frontier towns on her journey, Prudence no longer was convinced. With a toot, the train pulled away. She glanced back to see the caboose disappear from sight, leaving her stranded. The band of fear tightened around her chest.

I can leave on the next train.

But where would I go?

Prudence set her face to the future, allowing her fiancé to escort her down the dirt street. She picked up her skirt to keep the hem free of dust—not that it mattered—the dress was already dirty. She hoped Morgan's Crossing had sidewalks like a civilized town, but she didn't want to ask, for that would involve talking. Her chest was too tight for her to even breathe life into the words.

The strained silence stretched between them. They passed another couple, who nodded and smiled, glancing at her in curiosity, then several men, one after another.

One looked in desperate need of a bath. He leered at her.

Sickened, she glanced away.

Michael cleared his throat. "Take no notice of them, Miss Crawford. A new woman around here is a rare sight, and you mail-order brides have everyone curious."

At the mention of the other brides, she stiffened.

"I thought I'd find the platform crowded with your friends and their husbands, eager to attend your wedding."

"I was so busy getting ready to leave that I didn't write them." Prudence didn't want Michael to know about her strained relationship with the other women. She gave him a small smile. "Doesn't word spread fast in small towns? I assumed they'd know without my having to inform them."

"Word does spread fast. However, my understanding is your friends live on farms out of town, so although they knew of my intention to write to you, they didn't know when our marriage would take place. I only spoke with Reverend and Mrs. Norton a short time ago, but prior to today, I'd sent the minister a note informing him of the need to conduct a ceremony when you arrived."

She nodded, relieved to avoid talking about her "friends."

"Even though Morgan's Crossing is a two-day journey, we do have a teamster who makes regular rounds between our town and this one. El Davis services a few other out-of-the-way-places, as well. He brought me your letter and took mine to the minister." Michael made a sweeping gesture with his free arm. "So, you see, we are in touch with the larger world."

"I hardly think a teamster making the rounds constitutes *in touch*," Prudence said in a sharp tone.

Mr. Morgan stiffened.

Belatedly, she remembered Mrs. Seymour's advice to behave herself and scrambled for something to say without betraying more of her *difficult* character. After all, they weren't married yet, and Mr. Morgan could still draw back from the marriage. She didn't know what she'd do then. Throw herself on the mercy of one of the other brides? *I'd rather jump off a cliff.*

Perhaps if I think about what I'm grateful for. But nothing in this frontier town drew forth a feeling of appreciation.

In desperation, Prudence looked up. The sky gave her inspiration. Vivid blue arched overhead, sprinkled with a few cottony clouds. She supposed Darcy would have waxed lyrical, quoting some poem about nature. "Your sky is quite lovely, Mr. Morgan." In fact, she wished for a dress in the same hue.

One eyebrow lifted, and his mouth quirked. "I might own Morgan's Crossing, but the sky isn't one of *my* possessions."

She teetered on the brink of two different reactions—her normal defensive one, or allowing herself to go along with the humor in his eyes. *Honey, Prudence. Use honey.* "Do I hear a *yet*, Mr. Morgan?" she said archly.

"Have you discerned my ambition so quickly, Miss Crawford?"

"A man who owns a mining town must be ambitious—an admirable quality, in my opinion."

"I certainly agree." He waved his arm to indicate their surroundings. "Your friends must have told you about Sweetwater Springs."

Prudence gave a trill of false laughter. "We had many brides at the agency who settled all over the West. Letters constantly arrived from them. I'm afraid I never paid any mind to the ones from Sweetwater Springs. When your proposal came…why, I had such a whirlwind of activity to get ready to leave within a few days that I never thought to pull out those letters and reread them."

"I see."

"And actually, given the two-day journey between the towns, I didn't think that Sweetwater Springs would be that important." She smiled up at him and batted her eyelashes. "After all, *Morgan's Crossing* is to be my new home."

Mr. Morgan quirked his mouth into a smile that didn't reach his eyes. "You're right. Morgan's Crossing is important, as you will soon see for yourself."

She faked a small smile.

He gestured toward the white clapboard church. "I'm sure you know about Reverend and Mrs. Norton. I think you will like them. They are good people. Not at all stiff and judgmental like most clergy and their wives."

"I didn't know there were any other kind."

He chuckled.

Her heart rose at the sound.

"I agree. We do have a Catholic priest who makes his rounds to Morgan's Crossing about once a month. Father Fredrick. An amiable man. So you see, my dear Miss Crawford, kindly men of the cloth are one of our advantages."

"Kindly men of the cloth *who aren't around very often* are one of your advantages," Prudence said. Not until Michael laughed, did she realize with embarrassment that she'd spoken her thought aloud. *Oh, dear, I've put my foot in it now.*

He patted her hand. "I like how you think."

Relieved she hadn't alienated him with her improper disregard for Sunday service, Prudence resolved to keep silent the rest of the way to the parsonage by pretending to look around at the backwater town she couldn't care less about. *Surely I can hold my tongue until after the ceremony.*

They rounded the church to see a small one-story house set behind and to the right of the sanctuary. Prudence slowed her steps. *That's the parsonage?* Nothing like the roomy one back home where the minister of her church lived with his family. Of course, that dinky white church hadn't measured up either.

They mounted the steps and crossed the porch. But before they could knock, the door opened and a woman beamed at them. "My dear Miss Crawford, welcome to Sweetwater Springs." Her kind smile crinkled lines around her mouth and eyes. "I'm Mrs. Norton." She extended both hands to Prudence. "I'm thankful you've arrived safe and sound."

Stunned by the warmth of Mrs. Norton's greeting, Prudence placed her hands in the woman's.

Mrs. Norton squeezed them before releasing her. "Such a blessing to have you here."

Never before had Prudence been called a blessing. The idea made her uncomfortable—in a pleasant sort of way—and she didn't know what to say.

"I'm only sorry you won't be living nearby so we can develop a friendship."

Mrs. Norton's delight in Prudence's presence was a balm to the hurt and fear she'd suffered from Michael's unspoken rejection. She couldn't recall ever having such a welcome, and the comforting words soaked into her heart.

"But I know you will be such a gift to the people of Morgan's Crossing." She patted Mr. Morgan's shoulder. "She'll make you a happy man."

On the other side of the woman, Michael slanted an eyebrow in obvious skepticism.

The gesture pierced her good spirits. *My intended obviously doesn't agree with the minister's wife. We aren't getting off to a good start.*

"Come in and take some refreshment. I've been baking rolls, and we have plenty of butter and jam."

Prudence's stomach gurgled. "Sounds lovely." Unwilling to taste what passed for food at the various stations, she hadn't eaten in ages.

Mrs. Norton motioned them to follow her down a hallway. She gestured to a closed door they passed. "Reverend Norton is composing his Sunday sermon. Hopefully, he won't be long. He usually prefers to finish on Wednesdays, so he can give his full attention to his other duties without any worry over procrastinating." She shook her head. "But sometimes in a particularly busy week, the needs of our parishioners take precedence. A time or two, he's actually had to compose the sermon on Sunday morning."

"An admirable schedule," Mr. Morgan commented. "Wish more people possessed the same discipline. My shopkeeper is always submitting his accounts late."

He owns a store! Prudence had visions of shopping at the mercantile, purchasing whatever caught her fancy.

They entered the smallest kitchen Prudence had ever seen—not that she'd been in many kitchens before—crowded with a table, stove, and a counter with shelves above and below, a dry sink, a pie safe, and an icebox. On the far wall, a faded blue curtain screened a doorway.

A single window, partly open, let in sunlight. A breeze blew in the scent of a growing garden familiar now from her time at the agency, tilling, planting, and weeding under the tutelage of the gardener they called *the gnome.* A bowl of peas still in their pods sat on the table next to a long green zucchini and four plump tomatoes.

Rolls cooled on a tray on the stovetop. The smell of baking permeated the room and reminded Prudence of her failed attempts to best Bertha's biscuits. *One good thing about living in Morgan's Crossing—no one will compare my biscuits to that woman's.*

Mrs. Norton waved to a row of hooks by the door. "Make yourself comfortable, Miss Crawford."

Prudence divested herself of her traveling coat, relieved to take off the smoky garment, and hung it on a hook. *I can't wait to burn this.* She untied the ribbons of her hat and hung it on top of her coat. She smoothed her hair, which she wore in a plain bun.

Mrs. Norton frowned at Prudence's coat. "As soon as I've served you two, I'll take that outside and hang it on the clothesline. If I use the carpet beater on it, hopefully, the worst of the smoke and dust will be gone."

Prudence waved a dismissal. "Oh, don't bother. I plan to get rid of it."

"Oh, no, my dear. You'll have to wear it again on your way to Morgan's Crossing to protect your dress from the dust of the road."

Oh, no. "I hadn't thought of that," she murmured.

Mrs. Norton motioned for them to sit. "Would you like a cup of tea? Mrs. Carter kindly procures a supply for us when she orders tins from Boston. *Such* a treat. A lovely woman, Mrs. Carter. I'm only sorry you won't have a chance to meet her, Miss Crawford. And I know she'll be disappointed to miss your wedding. She attended Mrs. Flanigan and Mrs. Walker's ceremonies. The Carters are among our earliest settlers and have the largest ranch in these parts."

"Another time, perhaps," Prudence lied, not at all desirous of meeting someone who was friends with Trudy and Darcy.

Mrs. Norton busied herself in setting the rolls into a basket, which she placed on the table, along with dishes and knives, napkins, a small crock of butter, and a jar of red jam.

Hardly a refined presentation. But Prudence was hungry enough to make allowances for the woman not using small serving bowls for the butter and jam. She took a roll for herself before handing the basket to Michael, broke it open, and spread the two halves with butter. Impatiently, she waited a minute for the insides to cool, watching the golden butter melt into the fluffy dough.

Mrs. Norton fluttered her hands. "I'm sorry there's nobody here today to attend your wedding, Miss Crawford. I know you'll miss the support of Mrs. Flanigan, Mrs. Barrett, and Mrs. Walker at such an important time in your life."

Not one single bit. Prudence added jam to her roll and took a bite, savoring the yeasty taste and the tart sweetness of the strawberry jam.

"Are you sure you don't want to wait a day or two until your friends arrive?" Mrs. Norton gestured toward the curtained doorway. "You can use the bed in the lean-to for a couple of days."

Absolutely not!

"Your friends can all be informed by tomorrow, I'd say. I know they would make a special effort to attend."

They'd probably ignore the invitation. No sense letting Mr. Morgan and Mrs. Norton know how much we dislike each other.

"It's good to take advantage of friendships while you can. With living far away in Morgan's Crossing, you won't be seeing much of your friends." She shot Mr. Morgan an apologetic glance. "And from what Reverend Norton tells me, not many women reside in your town."

That suits me just fine. Mrs. Norton sounded too much like Mrs. Seymour, her outpouring of advice grating on Prudence's nerves. She had to restrain herself from screaming that she didn't want anything to do with those three women.

Mr. Morgan gave the minister's wife a charming smile, far warmer than any he'd directed at Prudence. "I like to think we have quality over quantity. My town has some good women who will welcome my wife with warm hearts and open arms."

Prudence squashed a wish that Michael Morgan was the one welcoming her with a warm heart and open arms. "We can't delay the wedding. Mr. Morgan is a busy man——" She threw the blame on him. "I'm sure he doesn't want to be away from Morgan's Crossing for too long."

"I'm willing to do whatever will make you comfortable, my dear Miss Crawford."

Prudence couldn't tell if he was being truthful or sarcastic, and she wished she could better discern her groom's character. She set aside the puzzle for another time. There'd be plenty of opportunity to learn to know Mr. Morgan. She had no intention of remaining in this tiny house any longer than she needed to. She wanted to marry and hurry to Morgan's Crossing and establish herself in her very own home.

Besides, Prudence suspected the longer they waited here, the more difficulty she'd have in remaining on her best behavior. She didn't want to slip and give her groom any reason to change his mind about marrying her. *I'd be the laughingstock of Sweetwater Springs.*

She remembered the stories of Heather Stanford, whose groom had refused to wed because his mother had faked his letter to the Mail-Order Bride agency. Heather had to work *three* jobs to support herself before Hayden Klinkner had given in, and they'd married. *I'd hate to have that happen to me.*

Prudence touched Mrs. Norton's arm. "Thank you for your kind invitation. But I feel it's best Mr. Morgan and I wed right away so we can start our new life together."

"Very well, my dear. Now then, let's get you ready for your wedding."

"Oh, if I could just use your bathing room. I'm desperately in need of a bath. I'd love a soak in a tub full of hot water."

Mrs. Norton pursed her mouth in a rueful expression. "I'm sorry, Miss Crawford. We don't have a bathing room. I have a half barrel that we fill with water and use on Saturday nights." She glanced at Michael. "We can chase Mr. Morgan and Reverend Norton out of the house, and I'll draw you a bath. It will take time to heat the water, though."

Prudence stared at the woman, too shocked to speak. Hypothetically, she'd known not everyone had indoor plumbing. But she'd never been in a home that didn't have a bathroom. The other brides had speculated about what primitive life in the frontier towns of the West might be like. But Prudence assumed that any house where she'd be living would have a bathroom and indoor plumbing, even ones she was just visiting.

Mr. Morgan pulled out a gold watch from the pocket in his vest, flicked open the lid, and glanced at the time. He shook his head, snapping the top closed and tucking the watch back into his pocket. "I hate to rush you, but unless you want to spend three days on the road instead of two, we must wed and be on our way."

"Oh, dear. That's true." Mrs. Norton pursed her lips. "I'll put some hot water on right away so you can at least wash up, Miss Crawford. While we're waiting, you can have a bite to eat. Mr. Morgan, can you see to her trunk?"

He cocked an eyebrow at Prudence. "You had four. Which one would you like?"

"The green one, please. I won't need the brown ones until later."

"My wagon will only fit two. You'll have to wait on the others and your barrel until El Davis can haul them to Morgan's Crossing.

Prudence frowned, hating the thought. But she supposed she could do without those trunks for a bit. Luckily, before she left the agency, she'd rearranged her possessions, packing items from most necessary to least necessary. She doubted in the next week or so there'd be much call for the two ball gowns she'd brought along. "On the brown trunks, next to my nameplate, you'll find a number. You can bring number one and the green trunk with us and leave the other two and the barrel for later."

He smiled and nodded in apparent approval. "You are very organized. I like that. Let me just polish off another of Mrs. Norton's fine rolls before I see to your trunks."

At least he's found something to like about me. I will say Mr. Morgan has polite manners.

Prudence wished the politeness wasn't just a veneer over the reluctance she sensed he was really feeling about marrying her. *Don't be silly*, she scolded. *You never expected to marry a man who was wild for you, anyway. You're about to obtain everything you wanted—a handsome husband, who's wealthy and influential, a mansion for a home, and townsfolk who'll envy your prestige.*

But at what price? That wasn't a question she'd asked herself before, and Prudence wasn't particularly pleased the doubt had popped into her brain now.

Mr. Morgan took his last bite, stood, and flashed a smile Mrs. Norton's way. "I wish my cook made rolls as good as yours. Thank you for the treat."

"I think you'll enjoy my rolls and biscuits, as well," Prudence said with pride, hoping to give him another incentive to like her.

This time his smile reached his eyes. "I'm glad to hear that."

Something fluttered within her stomach. Under the table, she placed her hand on her rib cage, safely warded by her corset. But Prudence was starting to suspect her heart might not be as well protected.

In the empty church, Michael waited in front of the altar for his bride, feeling as if pickaxes assaulted his innards. Reverend Norton stood next to him, holding a Bible or prayer book or some such volume.

Now I understand the proverb about being between a rock and a hard place. I'm squashed between a promise and a vow.

Michael knew he had faults. He wasn't always a good man. Many might consider him a tough man, and so he must be if he were to be successful. He needed plenty of gumption to manage a town full of miners, who often had heads as hard as the stone they worked.

Not only was he a man of his word, but Michael *valued* that quality about himself. Others counted on him standing steadfast—for good or for ill, depending on their opinion. If he were to forsake his promise to this woman, not only would he have broken his word, he'd have damaged his prized reputation, for the news had already spread around Morgan's Crossing that he was bringing back a wife.

He'd promised to wed Prudence Crawford. But now, in marrying her before God, he'd have more than his own word to uphold. He'd have the law of the land—and of Heaven—a heavy burden.

Reverend Norton cleared his throat. "It's good you are taking a wife. Morgan's Crossing has need of Miss Crawford, and you have need of a helpmate."

I have need of a wife, all right. But Prudence Crawford wasn't the one he'd had in mind. *Yet I'm marrying her.*

"When Mrs. Norton and I moved here after we were first married, we found Sweetwater Springs was even smaller than Morgan's Crossing is now. Instead of a bunch of miners, we had wild cowboys. And just as few women. My dear wife became quite a good influence on them all. In the early days, I credited her with bringing more men to church than did my preaching. We didn't have the piano at that time. But my wife's sweet face and her songs raised in praise to the Lord were quite a draw. She hasn't sung a solo for a long time. Claims her voice isn't what it was, although I don't agree."

Regretfully, Michael didn't sense any of Mrs. Norton's sweetness in Miss Crawford. Until this moment, he hadn't realized he even wanted that quality in a wife. *I should have composed a longer list of requirements for Mrs. Seymour.*

"I believe Miss Crawford will have a similar positive effect on Morgan's Crossing. And I will try to get out to your town more often." Reverend Norton sighed. "If only there were four of me to visit all the places in the region in need of a minister."

"We'll take you when we can get you, Reverend. I'm sure my wife will appreciate your efforts."

Michael heard the door open and turned to face the back of the church.

Mrs. Norton came inside, carrying a vase of white roses. She hurried up the aisle. "I told Miss Crawford to enter when she heard the music." She walked around them to place the vase on the altar. "I was determined your bride would have flowers, even if she couldn't have her friends present."

"I'm sure Miss Crawford appreciates your kind gesture."

She smiled and nodded. The faded blue flower on her black straw hat bobbed. "Do you have a particular choice of music you'd like me to play?"

Never having given the matter a thought, Michael shook his head, his mind blank. "I'm sure you'll pick something appropriate."

"Miss Crawford said the same thing when I asked her." She walked over to the piano bench, sat, and began to play, the notes filling the church.

Michael hadn't heard the piano played in years. There certainly wasn't one in Morgan's Crossing, not even in the saloon. The hymn sounded familiar from his childhood, but he couldn't place it. He wondered if Prudence had any musical training and if he should buy her a piano. Extravagant, yes—especially with the rest of the house to furnish with more sensible pieces. But he'd enjoy listening to music in the evening. *Might make doing the accounts easier.*

He had a sudden memory of his family sitting in a pew on Sunday, taking up the entire row, and wondered if he should have written them about his marriage. He didn't usually think about his parents and the myriad of siblings, nieces, and nephews he had. Growing up, he'd resented the competition for his parents' attention. The simple fact of having so many children meant wearing worn out hand-me-downs, envying other boys their slingshots, hoops, whistles, and shotguns. But now, he had an unexpected pang of longing for their boisterous love. *This marriage is making me maudlin.*

A shadow in the doorway of the church told Michael his bride had arrived. He girded himself, preparing to marry a woman he'd just as soon ship back to St. Louis.

Chapter Six

Although Prudence hadn't completely bathed from head to toe before the ceremony, a sponge bath had gone a long way in refreshing her spirits. Now, wearing a heavy silk gown in a shade of pale honey, she walked to the church with Mrs. Norton. When she'd chosen the dress, she liked how the color gave her eyes a golden glint, instead of washing her out like white or cream would have.

The gown had a simple cut, with a high rounded neckline and bustle with a short train, which she now carried looped over her arm to keep the skirt's hem off the dusty ground. In her other hand, she held a bouquet of white roses tied with a golden hair ribbon.

Mrs. Norton had adopted a motherly air toward Prudence. She'd ironed her dress and gathered the flowers while Prudence had washed up. Then she'd helped her into the gown.

I'd never thought to have such support on this day. Would my mother have been as attentive?

Maybe, but only out of relief from handing off her difficult daughter to become someone else's responsibility.

No, Prudence didn't miss her mother today, but with a pang of sorrow, she longed for Lissa's presence. Her sister probably would have married years before and had several children by now. Prudence didn't much care for children, but liked the thought of nieces and nephews who looked like her sister and, of course, who adored their aunt.

Sadness tightened her throat. *I didn't just lose Lissa, I lost the future families we would have woven together.*

Mrs. Norton carried a vase with more white roses. She glanced over. "I'm sorry you didn't have more of a chance to speak with Reverend Norton. I'm sure having the ceremony performed by an unfamiliar minister is one more unsettling experience for you."

"I don't mind. Reverend Norton seems quite kind."

The minister had surprised her with his warmth. The penetrating glance from his blue eyes seemed compassionate, not judgmental—so different from his Old-Testament-prophet appearance.

Normally when Prudence attended church, she never paid any mind to the minister's droning. Instead, during the sermon, she critiqued what every woman wore—mentally altering and redressing, ripping off trim from hats and completely refurbishing them.

The best part of church had been the opportunity to parade around in her latest outfit and covertly compare her dress to the new ones worn by her contemporaries. *One of the nice things about moving is having a whole wardrobe to show off, without spending a penny!*

With her free hand, Prudence ran her palm over the heavy silk of her dress and glanced around to see if anyone watched her. But she only saw a cowboy dismounting from his horse. He sauntered into a false-fronted building without noticing her.

They arrived at the church and climbed the steps.

Mrs. Norton touched her arm to stop her. "Wait until you hear the music, then come inside."

Prudence nodded.

Just outside the door, the minister's wife set the vase on the floor, reached for the back of the wedding gown, and let down the train, arranging the material in a fan shape. "Oh, you look beautiful, my dear."

Her misty eyes and sincere smile and tone made Prudence almost believe her.

Mrs. Norton picked up the vase and moved into the church.

Alone, Prudence noticed the trembling in her knees. She bit her lip and stood, just out of sight of the open door. In the silence, the thudding of her heart sounded loud enough for everyone to hear.

The piano music signaled her entrance.

This is it. She took as deep a breath as her tight corset would allow, inhaling the fragrance of the roses.

Head high, she stepped into the church, slowly moving up the aisle toward Mr. Morgan and Reverend Norton. The familiar music of "Blest Be the Tie that Binds" made sadness surge through her, remembering how Lissa loved to sing hymns in church, her sweet soprano soaring over the other voices.

Pressure built in her chest, and Prudence wanted to burst into tears. She hadn't cried since those terrible months after Lissa's death. In the years since, she'd stood dry-eyed through her parents' deaths and losing her home and possessions.

Does one ever stop mourning loved ones?

Fighting for control, she focused on Michael Morgan. Her groom was handsome enough to make her swoon, if only the stern-faced man would give her a genuine smile.

Prudence searched his face and saw no warmth, no joy in his expression. Inexplicably, her chest hurt again, the pressure building into her throat. *If I don't keep control, I will weep and shame myself.* She swallowed hard, not allowing herself to acknowledge the deep disappointment. After all, she'd never been like other women, dreaming about her wedding. Not since.... *No! I will not think of Lissa again.*

In that moment, Prudence realized her dreams had died with her sister. Grief welled within her, the *last* emotion she'd thought to feel today. But looking at Michael's impassive expression, the hard shell she'd grown around her heart after Lissa's death thickened another layer.

After returning to the parsonage following the ceremony, Michael detached his bride from the Nortons. He tucked her hand around his arm and led her to the wagon, which the livery stable owner had left in front of the church, with the horses hitched and ready to go. He wasn't looking forward to the long journey to Morgan's Crossing with this woman. *What will we even find to talk about?*

A breeze kicked up. Michael caught a whiff of his wife's perfume, light and floral and feminine. Different from the cloying scent the saloon girls at Rigsby's used to cover up a lack of bathing. No other woman in Morgan's Crossing could afford such an extravagance. He leaned closer and inhaled.

Maybe this marriage won't be so bad, after all.

Michael gave Prudence a warm glance. "I like that color on you."

After the ceremony, she'd changed into the same blue traveling dress, but hadn't yet donned the drab linen coat, and the fabric color shaded her eyes to blue.

He stared into them, fascinated by the transformation in hue before recalling his urgency to begin their journey. Michael waved toward the wagon. "Mrs. Morgan, let me lead you to the other side and help you up."

She glanced at him and smiled—not the tight turn of her lips he'd seen before, but with a sincerity that softened her features into almost prettiness.

"Mrs. Morgan," she said, her voice husky and pleasing. "I like my new name."

And I like the sound of you. He leaned closer and opened his mouth to say so, thinking he might follow the compliment with a kiss. But before he could do so, Prudence halted, staring past him.

"A wagon!" Her thin mouth turned down in a stubborn pout.

"Where's your buggy? Or a carriage? I certainly can't be expected to ride in *that* conveyance!"

Her sharp tone banished his attraction. Michael straightened, lowering his arm until she was forced to let go. "Of course, we need the wagon to transport your trunks." He used a sarcastic drawl. "I could hire the surrey from the livery, but you'll have to leave your possessions behind, taking only your satchel."

Her eyes widened, and her mouth opened.

"Don't worry. I've padded the seat to provide a cushion for your delicate bottom."

Red flooded her cheeks at his uncouth mention of her backside. She sniffed, raised her nose, and stalked past him to the side of the wagon.

Shaking his head, Michael cast his gaze to the heavens before following her. *This will be a long journey.*

Chapter Seven

After an hour passed in silence, sitting on the jolting wagon bench, Prudence sank into misery. They'd left the town behind, and she had nothing to do but stare at trees and prairie grass. She never imagined her wedding journey would take place in such an uncomfortable plebian vehicle.

And I have two days of this yet to endure. Prudence wasn't sure if she could bear it. *Once I arrive in Morgan's Crossing, I'll never want to leave.* With horror, she wondered if traveling back and forth to Sweetwater Springs would always be this tedious. The fear was enough to make her snap, "How do you usually journey when you come here from Morgan's Crossing?"

"She speaks." His mocking tone made it clear he was quoting from *Romeo and Juliet.*

Prudence silently filled in the rest of the words. *Yet she says nothing.* The hurt from his response ground like shards of glass into her heart. She held her tongue on the sharp words she wanted to slash out in return.

After all, she tried to reason with herself. *My question wasn't asked in honeyed tones.*

"I don't much, but when I do, I ride King, the bay on the left," Mr. Morgan said, his tone politer as he glanced sideways at her. "Do you ride?"

"I took lessons, of course. But there isn't much need to ride horses in the city." She wrinkled her nose, thinking of horse smells.

"Did you enjoy riding?"

"Of course not," Prudence responded, then paused when a memory hit her. She recalled the summers her family had spent in the country outside of St. Louis—she and Lissa exploring on horseback, Prudence on her pony and her sister on a gentle gelding. In retrospect, those golden summer days seemed idyllic—almost as if she'd experienced them in a dream, not real life. "Well, maybe…" She hesitated, unsure if she should confide more to this man—a stranger, even if he was her legal husband. *I don't have to tell him everything.*

"Maybe?"

"My sister and I used to ride together in the summer. We'd pack a picnic lunch and be gone all day." She smiled, remembering. "I'd forgotten how much we enjoyed ourselves."

"Sounds like you stopped riding."

"Lissa was ten years older. She became busy with her friends and rode with them. But they weren't interested in a child trailing after them, even when I graduated from a pony to a horse." Her throat clogged. After Lissa's death, her parents had sold their country house, including their mounts. The loss of her horse was the last time Prudence had cried. They hadn't even allowed her to say good-bye.

I've thought about Lissa more today than I have in the entire last month put together. Prudence wondered why, and then realized her life changed drastically today, just like everything had when Lissa died. Then the change had been heartbreaking and dreadful She'd been so sad and angry and resentful and afraid. *And alone.*

Surely, this marriage won't be dreadful. At least, I won't be alone.

But Prudence wasn't quite convinced. *Loneliness in a marriage would be far worse than the loneliness of being alone.*

After the longest drive of his life, Michael pulled up the team beside a tiny cabin—one of several along the road used as way stations between Sweetwater Springs and Morgan's Crossing. Anyone unlucky enough to become stranded between the cabins had to camp out in the open. Savvy travelers knew to bring supplies and gear in case weather or some other cause kept them from reaching safety. They also were sure to restock the wood they'd used and set a kindling fire in the fireplace for the next wayfarer.

They'd arrived just in time. The sun, flaming rose-red, dropped toward the mountainous horizon, casting orange and gold rays through the dusky purple sky. Darkness would soon fall.

Frowning, Prudence looked around. "Where are we?"

He tied off the reins, set the brake, and pointed to a fork in the road just ahead of their position. The other road veered off to the right. "If you traveled back that way, you'd also end up in Sweetwater Springs. It's a little-used track, not a direct route. However, it does go by the Barretts' place as well as the Walkers'. So that's the way we'd take when you want to visit them."

"Good to know," Prudence said in a noncommittal tone.

He gestured toward the cabin. "Our home away from home."

Apparent dismay filled her eyes. "Whatever do you mean?"

"A two days' journey," Michael reminded her. "We don't have hotels out here in the wilderness, so this will have to do. Unless you prefer to sleep in the open? I could make up a bed for you inside the wagon."

Her shoulders slumped. Prudence shook her head, causing a daisy on her hat to droop over the brim. Her expression was drawn, her eyes tired.

Michael found himself softening toward her. "Don't worry. There are several bunks. Your virtue is safe."

"My virtue is safe anyway," she uttered in stilted tones. "Part of the Mail-Order Brides of the West Agency agreement is that you wait a month to approach me for marital relations. You *are* a man of your word, are you not?"

Michael gritted his teeth on a growl, recalling the letter of terms he'd received from Mrs. Seymour, and frowned. At the time, he hadn't been pleased with the restrictions, but he'd been sure he'd seduce his new bride into seeing things his way. Now, he had little desire to bed this cold stick he'd married. *She can stay in her lonely bunk tonight for all I care.*

He winced at the thought, remembering how he'd looked forward to having a warm and loving woman to sleep with. *Hopefully, we'll muddle through to that point.* Then he remembered that his house only had one bed. He held in a groan. *Perhaps, Prudence and I will be on better terms tomorrow night!*

She looked askance at him.

"There's a creek in the back to wash up in. A privy..." His voice trailed off, as he remembered that the privy was just a hole dug into the ground and surrounded with rocks. Not the most comfortable spot to hang one's behind from. His bride was sure to set up a squawk when she saw the primitive toilet. In fact, she'd probably complain his ears off the whole time they were here.

Best try to head off her carping at the pass. "I'm sorry to say, the accommodations won't be what you're used to. Uh, what you *deserve*, my dear." He dipped his chin. "All I ask is that you bear with them until I can get you home. Will you do that for me?" He gazed into her eyes in an earnest appeal that was almost real.

She glanced from the house to him.

Michael kept a half smile on his face, the pleading in his eyes. He reached for her gloved hand and brought her fingers to his lips. "Please, my dear?"

"I'm not one to complain, Michael," Prudence said with a breathless hitch to her voice.

Still bent over her hand, he didn't point out her earlier reaction to the wagon. "You're a jewel among wives," he praised and straightened.

Her eyes narrowed.

Apparently I've gone too far. Hastily, Michael turned her hand, dropping a kiss on the exposed skin between her glove and sleeve. Liking the scent of her, he allowed his lips to linger, feeling her pulse skitter, while he inhaled one last floral whiff. He raised his head, looking into her eyes.

She stared back, mouth parted in obvious fascination.

Holding in his triumphant smile, he lowered her hand, giving the back a pat. "Stay right there, my dear, until I come around and help you." He made haste to jump down and move around the wagon. *Best get my bride washed up, fed, and in bed before she has time to react to her Spartan lodgings.*

On the other side of the wagon, Michael reached up for her, and guided her down, handling his bride as if she were made of spun glass.

She sent him a pleased smile, obviously liking his careful treatment.

"Make your way around the back." He pointed past the cabin. "You'll find the privy—a circle of rocks—and the creek where you can wash up. "I'll see to the horses and unload what we need for the night. Just let me know when it's safe to make an appearance."

Color flooded her cheeks, and she nodded.

"Good thing Mrs. Norton sent along a basket of food. We won't have to cook. I suspect you'd have found toiling over a fire in the fireplace, cooking some game I'd hunted, not to your liking."

Her chin snapped up. "Certainly not."

He reached into the wagon bed, pulled out her satchel, and handed it to her.

Grabbing the satchel to her chest, Prudence scurried away in the direction he'd indicated.

Michael waited until she'd rounded the cabin and was out of earshot before he let out the laugh he'd been holding in, pleased he'd figured out how to manipulate her. *Agency restrictions, indeed.* He'd maneuver around them easily. Once he got Prudence home, cleaned up, and settled into more comfortable surroundings, he had no doubt she'd be enjoying intimacy with him in their bed. *I'll bet on it.*

Chapter Eight

After church in Sweetwater Springs, the three mail-order brides and their husbands clustered together, talking. The couples had fallen into a routine of spending the first few minutes together doing a general catch up of news—crops, livestock, Jonah and Lina's little Adam—before the men would take themselves off, leaving their womenfolk to chat about more important things—such as *their husbands*.

All week, Darcy Walker looked forward to Sunday and the chance to mingle with her friends—both the other agency brides and those she'd met since moving here. As happy as she was in her marriage—and she knew Trudy and Lina felt similarly grateful—her two friends were her lifeline, helping anchor her in the community.

Before their marriage, Gideon had secluded himself in his forest home, and he hadn't made any friends except for the neighboring farmer and hunter Jonah Barrett. As his friendship with Lina, as well as Seth and Trudy Flanigan, deepened, he was able to feel comfortable in their presence.

She sent her husband, who stood by her side, an assessing glance, checking his comfort level.

Gideon's shoulders were relaxed. He watched little Adam Barrett with an indulgent smile as the toddler circled another boy about the same age, whose carrot-red hair curled around his head like a halo. As if sensing her attention, he turned to Darcy, and his smile widened into the one he only used with her.

Looking at him made a surge of love flood through her. *I'm so blessed.* Her husband knew how precious this short time in town was to her, so he did his best to fight his solitary nature.

Mrs. Norton drifted toward them, stopping to talk with other parishioners along the way, but steadily moving closer.

They widened their circle to let her in, each of them greeting her.

Mrs. Norton beamed her gentle smile. "My dears! I have such news for you!"

Blonde, blue-eyed Trudy touched the woman's shoulder. "Good news is always welcome. Don't keep us in suspense."

The minister's wife fluttered her hands. "I didn't have a chance to tell you before the service...your friend Prudence Crawford arrived yesterday to wed Mr. Morgan of Morgan's Crossing."

Her words dropped like stones into a lake, sending out ripples of shocked dismay.

Darcy's body chilled.

"Madonna Mia!" Lina rolled her eyes, but kept her face turned to Darcy and Trudy so Mrs. Norton couldn't see her expression.

Darcy saw Trudy struggle to keep her face blank.

The men didn't respond. They'd all heard "Prudence stories," but....

Mrs. Norton didn't notice their reaction. "Reverend Norton married the couple that very day. Considering her husband's business concerns, Miss Crawford didn't feel comfortable waiting until you all could attend the ceremony. So distressing to be married without the support of her friends."

We're not her friends! Darcy's eyes met Trudy's and Lina's. They knew exactly why Prudence hadn't waited.

"But she bade me convey her respects to you," Mrs. Norton continued.

I'll bet she did.

"I know Morgan's Crossing is quite a distance from us, but your friend is close enough that I'm sure there will be some occasions for you all to get together."

Darcy was the first to recover. "Thank you for the news, dear Mrs. Norton." *Should we tell her the truth?* She glanced at Trudy and Lina and could see the same dilemma in their eyes. She gave a slight shake of her head. Mrs. Norton's sweetness was legendary around town, even though in her role of a minister's wife, she must have often seen the dark side of life. The truth about Prudence's character would only distress the good-hearted woman.

With another flutter of her hands and a happy smile, Mrs. Norton left.

Again the couples closed their circle.

Gideon glanced at Darcy, a lift of an eyebrow conveying his concern. He knew she'd spent more time with Prudence than either Trudy or Lina. Since their encounter with Michael Morgan, she'd filled him in on many of them.

"Drat Prudence, anyway!" Darcy exclaimed.

A second silvery eyebrow rose to join the first, crinkling Gideon's forehead.

"That woman caused difficulties at the agency, and now she's causing difficulties here." Darcy sighed. "Well, she's causing difficulties in my *mind,* but only because I know it's just a matter of time before trouble trails in her wake and somehow involves Trudy, Lina, and me."

Gideon briefly placed his hand on her back in a silent gesture of support.

The warmth of his touch tingled through the layers of her clothing. Only recently had they discovered the sensual nature of their relationship, another way Gideon had changed her view of life. Their physical intimacy greatly enhanced their bond. After a lonely girlhood, Darcy had also learned of the simple comfort of holding hands or a hug. As usual, her husband had sensed just what she needed at the moment.

She reached for his hand, curling her fingers around his

work-roughened palm and allowing herself to relax. *I won't let thoughts of Prudence Crawford spoil this beautiful day with my husband and friends.*

Lina let out the groan she'd apparently been holding in. "What have we done? What have we unleashed on Morgan's Crossing?"

Trudy gave a sad shake of her head. "Those poor people of that town."

"As much as we all dislike the woman, we also had an instinctive distrust of Mr. Morgan," Darcy reminded them. "I'm tempted to ask, 'What have we unleashed on Prudence?'"

"Oh, I don't know." Lina shrugged. "I think Prudence can hold her own with the man."

Darcy thought of some of the hurtful barbs Prudence had directed Lina's way—about her accent, her Italian family, her curvy figure, her unmanageable curly hair, and her love of cooking. The woman had never been quite as cutting with Trudy and Darcy, who she seemed to view as her social equals. "Prudence certainly has the wherewithal," she agreed with Lina. "I'll really have to get that book now and send it to Mr. Morgan."

Gideon lifted his gray eyebrows. "What book?"

"*The Taming of the Shrew*," Darcy told him.

There was a split second of silence, then all three men burst into laughter.

"'Take this of me, Pru of my consolation—'" Gideon quoted, substituting Prudence's name for Kate's. His silvery eyes twinkled as he expounded. "'Hearing thy mildness praised in every town, thy virtues spoke of, and thy beauty sounded.'"

Looking at her husband made Darcy's heart warm. She placed a loving hand on Gideon's arm. "I think you are too positive, my dear. Yes, Petruchio was able to tame Katherine. But this isn't the Middle Ages, and I'm not so sure Prudence is tamable."

Trudy wrinkled her nose. "I never liked Petruchio."

"Me, neither," Darcy agreed. "I felt sorry for Kate to have to mold herself to such a man."

Trudy frowned. "We *can't* just send that book. Or at least not that one alone. That would be too cruel."

Seth laughed. "We certainly have enough of Trudy's extras. You can add a few more books and make them a wedding gift. Give us more space in the barn."

"Good idea," Darcy said. "We still have a box of Trudy's books at my house. I think we've read about half of them. I can take some of those and pack them around *The Taming of the Shrew*. Or should I put that one on top?"

They all laughed.

"On top," Trudy said, with a nod.

Her unusually tart tone made Darcy study her friend, who had never liked Prudence's harsh treatment of Evie. During her stay at the agency, Trudy had made friends with the servant girl and had been her stanch supporter.

Seth slipped an arm around his wife's waist.

Trudy leaned into her husband, glancing back to survey the congregation socializing in the shade of the oak tree. "I believe I saw El Davis here today. He's probably due to make a run to Morgan's Crossing soon."

Jonah glanced at Lina. "He can take the road by our houses that leads to Morgan's Crossing and pick up the box. That route's somewhat farther for him, but not much."

Problem solved.

Trudy frowned. "What will we do about the people of Morgan's Crossing? I feel for them."

Jonah glanced over at Adam, who was still taken with the other boy, before turning back to the group. "I've been to Morgan's Crossing before. There's nothing there but a mine and a saloon. There's barely a town."

Silence settled as they all thought of the ramifications.

Darcy bit her lip, pushing away the guilt, but some lingered. "That town doesn't sound like a place where we'd want our worst enemy to live."

Eyes wide, Trudy glanced at Darcy. "You forgot what she's done to us, as well as the other brides, especially Evie and Bertha.

Now that your half-brother *is* in jail, Prudence *is* our worst enemy, although I shouldn't call her an *enemy*. More like an *avoid-emy*."

Darcy lifted her chin. "This may be the making of her. Prudence has a choice to remain her same old disagreeable self, or she can change and become a better person."

Trudy pursed her lips. "Life in the West might be exactly what she needs."

This can be the making of Prudence, or this can be the breaking of her. "But still..." Darcy said slowly. "I believe we must give her a chance. Think of how much we've changed since moving to Montana Territory."

Gideon winked at her and thumped a finger on his chest. "Or how you made *us* change."

Lina's decisive nod made corkscrew tendrils bounce on her forehead. "This is true. What do you suggest?" She looked at Trudy. "Chickens?"

"Oh, dear no." Trudy's tone was adamant. "I'm not subjecting my chickens to Prudence's supervision. Remember how she attended the obligatory lesson at the hen house about caring for chickens and never returned?"

An idea sprouted in Darcy's mind. "Jonah, what's the setting of Morgan's Crossing?" She circled her arm to indicate the town. "As picturesque as Sweetwater Springs? Are there a lot of flowers? Trees?"

Jonah rubbed his bearded chin. "As I recall, there's mighty little growin' in Morgan's Crossing 'cept for paltry gardens and such."

"I have a suggestion," Darcy said on a happy note. "We'll send Prudence some seeds."

"Good idea." Trudy gave Darcy's shoulder a tap of agreement. "Too late to plant them now. But she'll have them for spring."

"We can gather the seeds at harvest time—" Lina chimed in "—and send them off once they're dried."

"Flowers, as well," Trudy added. "Maybe even some bulbs Prudence can plant now for the spring."

"That's it, then." Darcy said, feeling relief about contributing something that could aid both Prudence and others in Morgan's Crossing. "Hopefully, a need to create beauty around her will surpass her former reluctance to dirty her hands."

With an impish smile, Lina looked at Trudy and Darcy. "There's only one question?"

"What?" Darcy asked.

"Who will write Evie, Heather, and Kathryn the news?"

Dear Kathryn,

I have such news for you! We've ended up with Prudence Crawford in our vicinity, and we have no one but ourselves to blame! One Sunday, a man rode up to Trudy, Lina, and I while we were talking after church and blatantly looked us over, almost as if he were undressing us, or assessing us as if we were horses he intended to purchase. I'm surprised he didn't ask us to open our mouths and show him our teeth!

Then he said he was the mayor of Morgan's Crossing, a tiny town about two days' ride from Sweetwater Springs, and the owner of the mine there. He was looking for a wife, and now that our appearance had proven suitable, he intended to write Mrs. Seymour for a mail-order bride.

Kathryn, I must confess, the man set my back up. I told him to be sure and ask for Prudence Crawford. I know, so naughty of me. But the words just came out! Trudy and Lina had a similar reaction to his arrogance and played along. Really, we were quite wicked!

Only afterwards did we realize that if Mr. Morgan wrote to Prudence and she accepted, then she'd be living nearby to plague us. Well, as pride goeth before a fall, we are repaid for our actions, for Prudence married him. We didn't know until afterwards when Mrs. Norton broke the news to us, thinking we'd be delighted. How we kept straight faces, I don't know.

But since we received no notification from Prudence, we didn't have to attend the wedding, for we would have felt obligated to make an appearance. Apparently, she wants as little to do with us as we do with her. I don't know whether to feel sorry for Mr. Morgan, or think he's received his just desserts…as will she.

But enough of Prudence Crawford, or Mrs. Michael Morgan, as she now is. I want to hear all about what's going on. How's your Tobit? Has that nasty goat attacked you again? Has your memory returned completely? Any headaches? Are you keeping up with your piano practice, or are you too busy with being a farm wife? Have you taken on any students? None of us have heard from Heather or Evie for a bit. Those two are falling behind on their correspondence, and you have several letters to make up for from when you neglected me for so long because of your accident!

(I'm just teasing. I'm actually so very grateful you didn't suffer a more serious injury!)

As for me, Gideon and I are settled in the new house. I appreciate the larger space. Gideon and those who helped us rebuild managed to craft many of the same unique details that made his little cottage so delightful. Oh, Kathryn, I am truly blessed to have such lovely neighbors!

We have harvested our garden, which thankfully wasn't destroyed by the fire. Lina spent several days here with her dear little Adam, teaching me to can our fruits and vegetables. You can imagine how we laughed over all my mistakes! And I returned the favor, going to her house to help, although I really entertained Adam so she could work. I don't know what I would have done without her! I'm sure you've spent your time in a similar fashion. Did Heather and Mrs. Klinkner teach you how to can?

Almost every evening, Gideon and I walk to the pond, sit in the swing, and watch the sunset reflecting on the water. I wish I were an artist to paint such beautiful sights. I don't have to describe the scene to you, for I know you are also enjoying the beauty of Montana Territory. People back home don't know what they lack…although I do miss the ocean, and probably always will.

A few months ago, I could never have imagined such a life—dear female friends whom I will cherish forever, congenial neighbors who have become steadfast friends, and best of all, my devoted husband. Who could have dreamed such love lay in store for the six of us?

In rereading my letter, I've realized I used a lot of exclamation marks, and if my former governess were to read this, she'd severely chastise me. But Kathryn, my life is now full of emotion, and I've discarded many restrictions of my former existence, including punctuation rules!

Sincerely,
Darcy

Chapter Nine

The next day, Prudence sat on the hard bench seat of the wagon, stifling a yawn. They'd been up since dawn, and she hadn't slept well. *I've never been so bored in my life.*

She had to hold on to the side of the seat to keep herself steady as the wagon jounced over the rutted road, else Prudence would have crossed her arms over her chest in a fit of piqué. She'd started the morning so proud of herself for honoring Michael's request to bear with the dismal little cabin. *I didn't complain about the indignity of using those nasty rocks instead of a proper toilet, or sleeping on a narrow, hard bed with a straw mattress and no sheets, or eating the cold chicken Mrs. Norton provided with my hands instead of utensils....*

But the worst part of the evening was her intense awareness of her husband's every single move. He couldn't brush his hair off his forehead without her gaze tracking the lift of his arm or the flick of his hand. He'd been quiet, but she'd registered every word he'd spoken. Although exhausted, she'd taken ages to fall asleep, aware of the manly presence only a few feet away in the bed against the opposite wall.

What good is having a handsome husband if he ignores me? Perhaps I should have wished for someone ugly but attentive and adoring. Prudence pondered that idea, then concluded an ugly husband would be worse because she wouldn't want to look at him or be seen with him or have him touch her. *Someone in between, who adores me.* As if having a real conversation with herself, Prudence gave a decisive nod.

Michael caught the movement, turning to her and raising his eyebrows.

Warmth flushed her cheeks, and she scrambled for a topic of conversation to distract him. "Tell me...ah. Tell me of the people of your town. Mrs. Norton mentioned only a few women?"

"We have no single women, um, that is, no *decent* available women. Two saloon girls live there." He stumbled to a stop. "But they both have good hearts."

Prudence didn't chastise him for the improper mention of fallen women. *Mrs. Seymour would be so proud of me.* She wondered if he availed himself of the prostitutes' services but decided now wasn't the time to ask.

"That's why I decided on a mail-order bride."

Once again, the brief turn up of his lips seemed like a mechanical response rather than a genuine smile and hurt her heart.

"There's Mrs. Tisdale who cooks for me. Six miners are married. Most of the married women have children. One, Portia Rossmore, is in the family way."

"How many children?"

"Ten. We haven't lost any young ones lately, thank goodness."

Prudence shuddered at the thought, knowing all too well the pain families experience at such times.

He frowned. "Living with a bunch of uncouth miners won't be what you're used to, my dear. For the most part, however, they're good men. Some, especially my China men, have families living elsewhere, and they send home their pay. The Orientals pretty much stick to themselves. Sometimes trouble breaks out at Rigsby's, that's the saloon, when my men drink too much, get belligerent, fight, break some bottles and chairs."

"Oh, dear me," Prudence said, horrified. Her hand flew to cover her mouth.

"Don't you worry, now. You won't be frequenting the saloon, so none of this will affect you."

"What happens then? Are they arrested?"

He shook his head. "We don't have a sheriff, although I have guards for the mine that keep the peace if need be. Mostly the men patrol themselves. They grab the offenders and toss them in the river. That sobers them up right quick. Especially in winter."

Intrigued, Prudence chuckled.

Michael jerked and shot her a sideways look, as if surprised by her reaction. This time, his smile reached his eyes.

Her stomach twisted, and her heartbeat sped up. She couldn't help smiling back, wanting to strengthen this moment of accord. Greatly daring, Prudence briefly brushed her fingertips over the top of his thigh, reveling in the feeling of touching this man. *He's mine!*

Michael grinned. He transferred the reins to one hand and captured hers, kissing her fingertips.

Even through her gloves, she felt the press of his lips and the tingle that raced down her spine. "Mr. Morgan..." Prudence stammered to a stop, not certain of what she wanted to say.

"Must we be so formal? May I call you by your given name? And you call me by mine?"

"Of course, *Michael.*" Only a single word, yet using his name seemed so intimate. *Eventually there'll be more intimacies to come.* For the first time, the idea of being physical with a husband held some attraction, for she could explore these delicious feelings he aroused in her.

Maybe this marriage won't be so bad after all, Michael mused, once more allowing himself to hope. He flicked the reins to perk up the horses. Last night, Prudence had surprised him with her congenial attitude, proving she had more fortitude than he'd suspected. Although pleased he'd manipulated her so well, Michael was also weighed down by an unwelcome sense of responsibility toward her, of feeling shackled to a woman whose appearance and personality didn't appeal to him in the least.

But her bold touch on his leg and her unexpected husky laugh when he told of the drunken men and the river lightened some of the heaviness on his shoulders.

Laughter softened Prudence's countenance and brought light into her pale eyes. When he kissed her hand, the pink flushing her cheeks lent her the illusion of prettiness. He was surprisingly drawn to her—something Michael had doubted he'd ever feel from the first moment he'd laid eyes on her.

With a lighter spirit, he continued their conversation, describing the inhabitants of his town and telling Prudence humorous stories just to hear her laugh. He found himself enjoying the drive, and the time passed with them growing closer.

The shadows were deepening, and the sun dropping low when they started around the last hill before Morgan's Crossing. Soon the town would be in sight. He fell silent, realizing he was about to face the reckoning for his misleading letter.

In hindsight, Michael saw he'd made a horrible mistake in glossing over the realities of his home and his community. He'd been so focused on attracting the best wife he could that he hadn't thought through what would happen when he brought the woman home.

Now what do I do? Should I confess? Apologize? Try to skate through the situation as if nothing is wrong? He'd never been one for apologies, thinking they made a man look weak. And if he started with offering one, then Prudence would expect them throughout their marriage. He squirmed. *No apologies.*

Michael squinted at the sun's descent, wondering if he should slow the horses so they'd arrive in darkness—postpone the inevitable. But he was tired and wanted his supper, so he held the reins steady.

"How much longer?"

"Not far." He lifted his chin in the direction. "Once we're past this hill, you'll see the town in the distance."

Prudence gave a little bounce in her seat and clasped her hands together. "Oh, I can hardly wait," she said, her eyes shining.

Now Michael knew the saying about one's heart sinking was real, for his had just dropped to somewhere in the vicinity of his stomach. He opened his mouth to warn her but then clenched his teeth and stared straight ahead. *No sense in stirring the pot before the water boils. Maybe she won't think the place is so bad.* He'd wait and deal with her reaction when it came.

Chapter Ten

Prudence was so excited to arrive in the town she'd soon make her own, she practically bounced on the seat like a child. The hours of conversation she'd shared with Michael, the way his attitude toward her had warmed, the stories and mutual laughter, had banished her doubts about her husband. Whatever his initial reaction to her had been, he'd changed.

Her fantasies of being first lady of Morgan's Crossing returned, although this time she didn't imagine parading down the sidewalks of the town's main street on the arm of a faceless gentleman. No, now she imagined strolling, her hand crooked around the elbow of handsome Michael Morgan, so full of happiness that she practically floated.

Lost in her daydream, Prudence didn't mind that her husband had fallen silent. The wagon wheel jolted over a rock, making her buttocks ache and bringing her to an awareness of her surroundings. When she'd asked, "How much longer?" she listened to his directions, leaning to the right as if to peer around the hill and view the town more quickly. In her impatience, each turn of the wheels, every hoof beat, seemed too slow.

Finally, they cleared the hill. Prudence squinted but didn't see the expected town—no tall trees around a town square, no multi-storied buildings, no flag flying atop a high pole in front of a stone courthouse, no church steeple rising into the sky. Wondering if the sun's rays blocked her view, she raised a hand to shield her eyes. *Still nothing.* After a while, her arm became tired, and she lowered her hand, struggling to curb her anticipation.

They came to a wide river, bigger than the streams they'd crossed so far. A wooden bridge with low railings spanned the water, the first sign of civilization she'd seen all day. With a clatter of hoof beats and rattling wheels, the wagon crossed the bridge. She pointed toward the water. "Is this the reason for the name of the town?"

"Partly. Before I built the bridge two years ago, this was the only ford for miles. But there's also another river on the other side of the town, which crosses this one about half a mile downstream. The town's built between the two. Nice fishing in these waters. Best trout you'll ever eat."

She playfully winkled her nose. "I'll have to take your word for it."

He grinned. "I don't have much time for fishing, but I'll take you one day."

"Me?" This time her nose-wrinkle wasn't playful. "Why ever would I want to *fish?*"

The grin fell away from his face. "Forget I mentioned it."

Prudence bit her lip, regretting her hasty response, but not sure how to mend the rift that had just re-opened between them. For the first time, she saw the truth of Mrs. Seymour's warning and realized how easily she could damage this new relationship that she was already coming to cherish. *But really, fishing? What else could I have said?*

Best not say anything. Prudence sat back in her seat, schooling herself to respond positively to Morgan's Crossing. She knew everything wouldn't be to her taste but told herself to ignore those things and focus on what she did like. *Gratitude,* she reminded herself.

"There's the town." His tone was stiff and muted.

Tiny buildings came into sight. Prudence straightened, trying to see more clearly. *Surely they should be bigger and there should be more of them.*

We're still too far away, she reassured herself. *I'll be able to see more detail in a few minutes.*

But as they drove closer, Prudence failed to see the rows of structures she sought. Her stomach tightened in dread, and her heart beat slow, heavy thumps against her ribs. She pressed her lips together, refusing to give up the tattered remnants of hope.

The road divided, one fork heading toward the town and the other snaking around a low hill.

Michael jerked his head to the left, toward a hill that in Missouri would probably be described as a mountain. In the distance, the dark purple-gray mountains loomed far larger, though. "The mine's up there. I'll take you to see it tomorrow."

Gasping, she turned to stare. "You mean go inside?"

He nodded.

Prudence couldn't imagine herself doing any such thing. But if she was to be the owner's wife, perhaps a tour was in order at some point in the future.

The closer they came to the cluster of buildings, the tighter her stomach knotted. As the horses veered toward the right, Prudence saw a two-story gray Queen Anne with burgundy trim and a wide white porch, and she relaxed. Although the home would be on the nice side of ordinary in St. Louis, from what she'd seen of Montana Territory, the dwelling was far more fashionable than most, even those in Sweetwater Springs.

Her fears eased. With houses like that in the town, Michael's home would, indeed, be a mansion.

Once on the street leading between the buildings, Prudence could see the remaining ramshackle structures, and her body vibrated in horror. *Why, this is no more than a mining camp!*

Frantically she looked around for the mansion, but no other house was in view. She couldn't count the shacks as actual homes, as they were barely more than boxes that sprouted like misshapen mushrooms on either side of the street. A row of canvas tents lined the far end of the road. Rigsby's Saloon was easy to spot. A store. A building that could be a church or school, and the large two-story rectangular structure with a porch on the front.

That can't be Michael's house? Before she could exclaim, Prudence remembered he'd said his home was new. Relieved, she twisted in her seat, searching for the mansion, wondering if it was built of brick, stone, or wood.

Michael drew up the wagon in front of the gray house. "We're here, my dear," he said in a hearty tone.

Horrified, she glanced from his face to the house. "You wrote that you lived in a mansion." Her voice rose, and she jerked out a rigid hand as if to hold back the truth. "That is *not* a *mansion.*" She practically screamed the last sentence.

He winced. Disappointment flicked in his eyes, quickly hidden by a sardonic expression. Michael waved his hand. "Look around you, my dear. In comparison, is not my home—now *your* home—a veritable mansion?"

Disappointment and anger curdled in her stomach, nauseating Prudence.

A shout from down the street had men spilling from the saloon and rushing toward them. Two women in low-cut dresses that ended at their knees joined the crowd. *Scandalous.*

Some men detached from the throng and raced in the other direction toward the cabins. Women, some carrying babies, a few with children at their sides, hurried from those houses, joining their menfolk in the tide of people headed their way.

Alarmed, Prudence watched the flood of men in rough clothing approach, laughing and shouting questions and comments to Michael, calling him *boss.* Never in her worst nightmares had she imagined her arrival in Morgan's Crossing to be like this.

The crowd of people surrounded the wagon. A gust of wind brought the smell of unwashed bodies her way.

Instinctively, she grimaced, lifting her hand to cover her nose.

The men's grins fell off their faces, and the laughter died to silence.

"Now you've done it," Michael said in an undertone.

The injustice of that remark stung. *I've been so good on this trip—exercised all my self-control!* She lowered her hand. *"I've* done what?" she snapped.

"Hush now."

Prudence paid his admonition no mind. "You *lied* to me, Michael Morgan. Wrote me *false* information. Perjured yourself."

"So shoot me," he growled.

"Give me your gun and I will."

"And leave you a rich widow?"

"Rich, ha." Prudence poured scorn into her words, the wide sweep of her arm encompassing the town. "You call living like this *rich?* Beggars in St. Louis live better." Her gaze settled on the crowd.

The baleful stares of the men made her shiver. *Why are they blaming me, when this is all his fault?*

Michael cast her a darkening glance before surveying his townsfolk and flashing a charming smile. He reached for her hand.

To think I'd almost fallen for that smile! She tried to pull away.

He tightened his grip, immobilizing her arm. "Let me introduce my wife, Prudence Morgan. You'll have to excuse her. My dear bride has had a long journey. She's exhausted and *not* herself."

Incensed by the way Michael poured his lies over them, Prudence shifted on the seat, preparing to kick his ankle.

"Leave us some privacy." Smiling to include the whole group, he winked.

Prudence gasped, cocking her foot, only to have her heel catch in her hem. She reached down to untangle herself.

"We'll host a party tomorrow night for you all. You'll have the opportunity to welcome my sweet bride." He glanced at her with a smile that would make honey melt.

Only she could see the disdain in his eyes. The shock of Michael's invitation made Prudence drop her foot. *A party? For tomorrow? For all these people? Didn't he know a successful party takes weeks of planning?*

Michael made a gesture of dismissal.

With a few mutters and sideways glances in her direction, the men left, and the women followed.

Only one older woman with snow-white hair stood firm, her arms akimbo on her plump waist. "Mr. Morgan, whatever do you mean you're giving a party tomorrow?" she asked in a tart voice. "You'd better have loads of supplies in that wagon, else I've no idea how you're feeding the whole town."

Prudence felt an immediate bond of kinship with this woman—that is, until her words soaked in. "You mean there's not enough food for a party?" She glared at her husband. "How could you do this to me?"

He hunched his shoulders and had the grace to look sheepish. "I didn't think things through."

Prudence almost softened.

"I was attempting to prevent a mass judgment against your holding your nose at them."

"They *smelled*." Prudence glanced at the woman, realizing she'd probably just offended her, too.

The woman's stern face broke into a smile that crinkled her skin. "That they do," she agreed. "And so I've told them many a time."

Relieved, Prudence smiled at her.

"*My* son is not allowed to cross the threshold of our house—at least on warm days—without first washing up. And regular baths every Saturday, for all he complains about haulin' water for the tub." She shot a pointed glance at Michael. "Indeed, and I've told you this town needs a bathhouse."

Bathhouse? Prudence eyed the dinky cabins, for the first time seeing the privies behind them. Holding her breath, she glanced over at the gray house. *Please, please may there be a bathroom. I long for a hot soak!*

The woman smiled at Prudence. "The tub's already filled with hot water. I figured you'd arrive about now. Should still be comfortably warm."

"Thank you." Prudence still wasn't sure if the woman was

talking about a tub in a bathroom or not. She almost hated to ask.

Michael glanced back and forth between the two of them. "Mrs. Morgan, I'd like you to meet my cook, Mrs. Tisdale."

The woman smiled and nodded. "You'll find your supper all ready and warming in the oven. Only rabbit stew, I'm afraid, just in case you arrived late. I didn't want any other dish to spoil."

Rabbit stew? Prudence stiffened. She'd never eaten such a thing.

Mrs. Tisdale gave a decisive nod. "If you arrived late, I knew you could do a quick heat up of the pot without a problem. I also made a wedding cake to mark the occasion."

The smile and the mention of a wedding cake brought tears to Prudence's eyes. Why this woman, a servant really, had that effect on her, she didn't know. After all, Mrs. Tisdale was just doing her job. But the woman had stood up to Michael about the party, risking being fired. "So thoughtful. Thank you."

"Today, Mrs. Rivera and I took the liberty of stripping the bed and washing the sheets. We also dusted and swept the floors."

Michael leaned closer to Prudence. "When I need her to, Mrs. Rivera cleans the house and does the laundry."

"When you need her to?" Prudence echoed, not sure what he meant. *Doesn't the house need cleaning every day? And laundry done weekly?*

"'Bout every couple of weeks."

"Every couple of weeks?" To her ears, her voice sounded faint with disbelief.

Michael looked at Prudence, his gaze hard. "Now that you're here, *my dear*, there will be no need for Mrs. Rivera's laundry service, nor for Mrs. Tisdale to cook for me."

Prudence glared at him in shock, then glanced at Mrs. Tisdale and saw her anxious expression. The woman obviously needed the work.

Her resolve hardened. She would not allow this man to *boss* her around and dismiss the only servants she apparently had.

Best begin as I mean to go. Prudence lifted her chin. "You were the one who invited the whole town to a *party*. Imagine how they will feel tomorrow night when they see the *empty table* because your bride refused to allow you to treat her like a slave."

She has me over a barrel. Michael stared at his wife, annoyed that she'd caused him to lose his composure and utter such an inane statement about cooking, which had only gotten him in trouble. Inwardly, he stared at a proverbial fork in the road, knowing he could compound his stupidity and force Prudence to handle the cooking for the party, or he could back down and admit he'd made a mistake. But if he did so, he'd be letting her win—not a good precedent to establish with their new marriage.

Thank goodness I hadn't actually committed to firing Mrs. Tisdale—for if I had, I'd have to stick to my word. Michael had intended to ascertain the quality of his wife's cooking skills before figuring out what to do with Mrs. Tisdale. He glowered at both women. "It's late and I'm tired. We'll discuss everything in the morning."

Mrs. Tisdale gave Prudence a commiserating glance, which only served to further irritate Michael. He would not have his wife conspiring with his employees against him.

Bah. I'm becoming over-fanciful.

He climbed down from the wagon and looked around for his stableman.

Howie Brungar, long and lean, slunk from the shadows at the side of the porch and ambled over.

"Bring my wife's trunks inside. Carry them to the bedroom." Michael's order came out curter than he'd intended. He took a deep breath and moved to the other side of the wagon to help Prudence down.

She accepted his hand but avoided eye contact.

Howie began to unload the wagon.

Michael clenched his jaw. This should have been a triumphant moment—bringing home his bride to his new house, acquiring a first lady for Morgan's Crossing. Instead, their homecoming lay in shambles, and he'd no idea how to make things right. He might not be attracted to Prudence, would prefer another woman over the one he'd ended up with, but he was tied to her now and needed to make the best of the situation.

His wife extended a hand to Mrs. Tisdale. "I'm so delighted to meet you. Thank you for bringing supper over. I'm famished."

"You're very welcome, Mrs. Morgan. You'll find the tub in the bedroom. All you have to do is add more hot water."

Prudence released Mrs. Tisdale's hand and swung to face him. "Do you mean to tell me you have no bathing room?"

With a mental curse, Michael held up his hands in a placating gesture. "Ah, to be correct, *Mrs. Tisdale* told you we have no bathing room."

"Do *not* equivocate with me, Michael Morgan." Her tone sounded sharp-edged, on the verge of hysterical.

He bit back a retort.

"Do you have indoor plumbing?" With her forefinger, Prudence made an angry downward slash at him.

"You'll be pleased to know there's a pump in the kitchen sink."

"What about an indoor toilet?"

He shook his head. "Perhaps in the future. Right now, there's an outhouse."

"Oh, dear Lord." Prudence glanced down the road, as if assessing leaving. Her face reddened, and fire flashed in her eyes. She looked like a kettle full of steam about to explode.

I'd better get her inside first.

Howie moseyed out of the house and gave him a sharp salute to indicate he'd finished his assignment.

"See to the horses." Michael grabbed Prudence's elbow. "Come into your new home, my dear."

She wrenched her elbow away.

He sighed, doubting the rest of the evening would be any easier.

Chapter Eleven

In a second obvious attempt to maneuver her into the house, Michael offered his elbow to escort Prudence up the steps, apparently pretending this was a normal homecoming.

She ignored him, simmering with anger and disappointment—not just from discovering the reality of Morgan's Crossing, but because she'd felt so happy, enjoying the conversation with her handsome husband and anticipating the arrival at her new home. Even the indignity of having to use a bush for a toilet on their journey hadn't done much more than elicit some mental complaints, which she virtuously hadn't expressed to Michael.

Joyous. Yes that is the word for how I felt today. Lifting her skirts, she trudged up the steps, her legs weighed down.

Prudence realized she'd just lost more than her imaginary home. *I lost the hope growing in my heart that, for the first time since Lissa died, life would be different. I would be different—lighter, contented, even amiable.* She almost snorted at that last word, only ladies didn't snort, so with difficulty, she suppressed her reaction.

Michael opened one of the outer double doors. Glass gleamed in the upper halves. "Welcome to your new home, my dear."

He doesn't sound at all welcoming. Quite the contrary. Stung by his sarcastic tone, Prudence ignored the man, sailing past him as if he were no more than a butler. Inside the small vestibule, she waited for him to pass and open a second set of doors, also with glass panes.

From the corner of her eye, she saw Michael open both inner doors with a dramatic flourish. He bowed and straightened with a sweeping wave of his arm to usher her in.

Prudence turned her head just enough so he could see the roll of her eyes, showing what she thought of his theatrics. Then she looked straight ahead and glided past him into the entryway.

In the shadows from the deepening dusk outside, the entry looked spacious enough. An oil lamp burned on a small table across from a straight staircase that widened the last few steps to the floor, the banister curling into a spiral. *Satisfactory.*

"Well, what do you think?" Michael asked, with a hint of anxiousness in his tone.

I don't care about his feelings. Prudence gave a mental shrug. "I prefer curving staircases." She flicked a glance at him to see his reaction to her criticism.

"I see." His voice sounded bland. He jerked his thumb toward the right. "The parlor."

Prudence moved to the small table and picked up the oil lamp, realizing how much she would miss gaslight and the electricity that had recently come to St. Louis. Holding the lamp in front of her, she walked into the parlor, wishing the room were the size of the double one at the agency.

In the small circle of light, she saw a large settee, with what looked like blue velvet cushions. She liked the color, but wasn't about to say so. A worn leather armchair looked out of place next to the settee. Prudence glanced around but didn't see additional items of furniture. Raising the lamp, she slowly pivoted, peering into the corners of the room, but saw only a round stove on the opposite wall.

Michael remained where he was. "I did mention in my letter that you'd be selecting the furniture."

"Another equivocation," she said in a chilled tone, lowering the lamp. "I must say, these last few minutes have given me illuminating insight into your true character."

"I believe I'll say the same." Michael matched her coldness.

Prudence jerked up her chin, gesturing for them to leave the parlor and see more of the house.

"My study is across the way." He turned without waiting for her, strode through the entry, and to the other side.

With another eye roll at his rudeness, Prudence followed him. In the study, she caught sight of bookcases on both sides of a fireplace with forest green tiles. She sniffed the smell of stew and frowned at the realization that the kitchen must be uncomfortably close.

She raised the lamp, throwing light over the empty shelves. *Are all his books packed away for some reason?* Although her housekeeping studies at the agency had kept her too busy to read, when she still had lived at home, she preferred to spend time reading rather than socializing. With a stab of regret, she thought of her parents' library—a room of floor-to-ceiling bookshelves overflowing with volumes, some first editions. "Where are your books?"

"They have yet to be acquired. I'd hoped you'd bring along some like your friend Trudy Flanigan did."

"Trudy brought practically the whole contents of her father's home," Prudence snapped to hide a stab of sadness. "I'm traveling far lighter." She had no intention of telling him about her family's shameful losses.

Thank goodness I've brought a few books with me. She'd held on to the Louisa May Alcott stories both she and Lissa had enjoyed, as well as some of her favorite novels. But she'd left many of her personal books behind, thinking them easily replaced. *I should have left the ball gowns and brought more books.*

"I do have several of my favorite novels with me. Enough to fill half a shelf."

"Novels," he scoffed.

"If you wanted a scholarly wife, you should have written earlier and married Darcy," Prudence said in a light tone. "Then again, Darcy's reading level would be quite above your own, so it's just as well you didn't."

Her dig penetrated. Michael firmed his mouth before looking away. "At least she would have brought me wealth."

His barb hit, yet Prudence didn't let him see. "You're the owner of a gold mine," she mocked. "You're supposed to have wealth. Or was that gold dust just for show."

"You have it precisely, my dear." He waved a hand up and down the length of her body. "And my plan worked. *Lucky me.*" His tone said the opposite.

She stifled a gasp and glanced away, trying to regroup for another round. Never before had anyone bested her in a verbal war, certainly not her parents. Her father would retreat to silence, her mother to tears. Early on, Prudence had driven away any potential female friends. The women at the agency tended to avoid her, although from time to time one found the backbone to remonstrate with her.

This verbal war hurt, yet stimulated, her—the pain-filled energy crackling between them. Prudence didn't know what to think about their interactions. She glanced away, her gaze falling on the empty bookshelves. *What if he's illiterate?* Her body stiffened. *He could have lied about his education, as well.* She gazed at him in disgust. "Do you not read?"

"I don't have time to read," Michael said defensively. "I own businesses. I spend my time going over the accounts."

Accounts. That means he's familiar with numbers. So he must be educated.

Prudence relaxed her rigid shoulders and turned to survey the rest of the room. The study, too, lacked furniture. Only a fine desk took up some space, with a wide-armed wooden chair behind it, a ladder-back chair to one side, as if someone had drawn it up to the desk to work beside him. She wrinkled her brow. *What is that on top?* She walked over to survey the surface of the desk and saw two place settings of tin dishes, with jam jars for glasses. A pewter inkwell and pen was pushed to one corner.

A cheesecloth-covered pot sat on a crocheted yarn doily. Next to the pot was another cheesecloth-covered mound. "What is this?" Without waiting for an answer, she lifted the edge to see a three-layer cake. *How odd.* "Why didn't Mrs. Tisdale use the dining room?" For the first time since entering the room, she looked directly at Michael.

A guilty expression crossed his face.

"*Michael Morgan*," she warned. "Tell me what is going on here."

"I told you about furnishing the house. That includes a dining room table and chairs."

"What?" Prudence gaped at him. "Where have you been eating?" She shook her head, her gaze on the desk, the answer obvious. "But why?"

He let out an audible breath. "Because I've been too busy. Because with just me, I only needed the basics. Because I wanted my wife to choose items to her taste."

At least his answers made sense, and Prudence couldn't fault him for allowing her to select what she wanted. She stared down at the cake—vanilla or lemon? In the dim light, she couldn't tell for sure. Probably vanilla. Lemons would be hard to obtain in this out-of-the-way place.

A sudden thought made her jerk up her head to stare at him. "Michael, you invited everyone to a party tomorrow night. Where will you put them? There isn't even a table to set out food!"

He stared at her in obvious consternation. "Damn, woman. You're right."

The curse hung in the air between them. Prudence didn't know whether to chide him for daring to assault her ears with course language or join him with letting out a few improper words she'd heard on the streets of St. Louis. *Maybe I should do both.*

Caught up in the dilemma, she did neither. Somehow, Prudence suspected this wouldn't be the first time she felt jammed between twisted responses to her new husband.

Michael stared at his wife, ashamed for having just lost control over his foul mouth. He'd been around miners for too long, learning to cuss with the best of them. Sometimes he had to speak their language to get his point across. Until this minute, he hadn't thought about how much his manners—no, his whole outlook—had changed.

If he were still a boy, his father would tan his backside for daring to curse in front of a lady, or his mother would seize his ear and drag him to the sink where she'd wash his mouth out with soap for using foul language. *I'm married now. I'll have to be careful.* But he suspected his bride would severely try his resolve.

The echo of his parents' disappointment still ringing in his ears made Michael groan. He ran his fingers through his hair. "I apologize. I was wrong to speak so."

Her eyes widened as if he'd surprised her, and he wondered why. *Perhaps she senses how rare an apology is for me.*

"Thank you." Prudence's expression puckered. "What else is missing in this house? Please tell me there are beds."

"*A* bed."

Her eyes narrowed. "What do you mean?" Her voice held a threatening note. His wife took a step toward him, looking like she might bash him over the head with the lamp.

Not that I can blame her. The tour of his house was not going as he'd planned.

"Where will *you* sleep?"

Michael flashed the smile he'd always used to charm the ladies. "In the bed with you, my dear."

Scowling, she took a step back. "You do recall the agency terms?"

All too well. "I'd hoped you'd agree to waive them." His wife would become more docile once he bedded her. He was confident in his ability to pleasure a woman—although he'd not done so for far too long—and how, afterwards, she'd become more attached to him. *Annoying at the time, but now part of my calculated plan.* "I promise you'll enjoy the experience."

She lifted one shoulder. "I've already endured enough of your promises. I'm not such a fool that I'll fall for them twice. No. I'll take the bed." With an airy flick of her wrist, Prudence dispensed with him. "You'll have to find somewhere else to sleep."

Visions of moving back to his cabin, of the gossip racing around town.... *Oh, no. I'm sleeping in my own bed.*

Time for my charming smile again. "If you allow me to introduce you to some of the pleasures of intimacy—" he coaxed, extending a hand toward her "—I believe you'll enjoy the experience enough to want to go further and consummate our marriage."

"Consummate," Prudence slowly repeated the word as if thinking about what he'd said.

Michael's hopes rose.

His bride glared at his outstretched hand. "I'll have to meet with a lawyer, but I believe at this point our marriage can be annulled without much ado."

Her words shocked him. If Prudence followed through with an annulment, she'd make him the laughingstock of his own town. Of Sweetwater Springs, as well. He scrambled for some way to deflect the idea from her mind—*at least until I can seduce her.* "I suppose I could sleep on the settee," Michael said grudgingly, giving in for the moment. "Or on a temporary pallet in one of the other bedrooms."

She nodded.

But instead of the triumph he'd expected, she looked tired, as if he'd beaten the stuffing out of her. *And in a way, I suppose, I have.* Feeling guilty, yet not wanting to think of himself as such a scoundrel, Michael glanced at the food set out on the desk and realized he was famished. "Would you prefer to see the rest of the house, or go ahead and eat?" He glanced at the doorway. "Well, I guess you'd first like to use the privy and wash up."

Prudence rolled her eyes.

That makes three times she's done that. He'd have to speak to her about continuing to use such a childish gesture to express her disdainful thoughts. *Perhaps I'll forbid her to roll her eyes at me.* But as quickly as he toyed with the idea, Michael realized the order would cause Prudence to do the very thing he'd just forbidden. Hastily, he decided to exert his husbandly authority over another matter.

"Let me show you to the kitchen." He extended his arm. "The back door leads outside. You'll find the privy there."

"I can't believe there's not a bathroom," she muttered, shooting him an angry look. "You should have warned me about this benighted place."

"You should have warned me I'd be marrying a shrew." He drawled the words.

Prudence jerked back as if he'd struck her.

Once again, guilt clenched his stomach.

His wife glared and balled her free hand.

At the sight, his brief spurt of guilt vanished.

"Why, Michael Morgan," her honeyed tone mocked. Relaxing her fist, Prudence fluttered her hand to touch her chest. "You call *me* shrewish?"

"I did, my dear."

"Why, my *dear* husband." Her tone cut. "You haven't seen shrewishness yet. Oh, no, not in the least. But I'll show you shrewishness, yes, I will." Her smile was as sharp as her tone. "Just you wait."

Chapter Twelve

After a surprisingly tasty supper, which Prudence attacked as if she'd just lived through a famine—in a ladylike way, of course— she climbed the stairs to the second floor, bunching the fabric of her skirt in one hand and carrying the lamp in the other, her traveling coat folded over her arm.

Earlier, Michael had shown her the three upstairs bedrooms, two of them completely unfurnished, although he assured her he'd already ordered a bed for the guest room, so Father Frederick could stay in comfort when his rounds brought him to Morgan's Crossing.

With the heels of her shoes clicking on the polished wide-plank floors, Prudence followed the hallway into her bedroom— about the size of a guestroom at her parents' house. Aside from her trunks and satchel, and the tin tub in front of a navy-blue tiled fireplace, only a four-poster bed and a slatted crate holding folded clothing stood in the room—no wardrobe, washstand, dressing table, bureau, or bedside tables. A window nook— shaped like half of an octagon—peeked over what Michael had said was the back garden.

Prudence could imagine tucking a comfortable chair and a small table there, where she'd take tea, read, or do handwork. An annoying husband wasn't anywhere in that cozy picture.

Feeling wistful, she set her lamp on a trunk, hung the coat over one of the bedposts, and walked over to stand at the dark windows, bare of curtains, the perfect backdrop for her imagination. Perhaps if this house were magically transported to the country outside St. Louis, where she could've lived alone— although, of course, servants silently arrived, did their work out of her sight, and left Prudence to her own devices—she might just find contentment.

For a woman living alone, the size of this house was actually perfect. Her lips curved. She reached out and placed her palm on the white woodwork of the window frame. *Mine.*

The sound of footsteps coming her way down the hall broke her reverie. With a sigh, Prudence turned and looked toward the open door.

She saw a faint glow of light before Michael entered, carrying a second lamp.

With an eyebrow cocked, he glanced around.

She followed his gaze, again seeing the emptiness of the room.

"I came to see if you needed anything."

"Anything?" Prudence said tartly. Her arm swept the room. "As you can see, I'm in need of a great deal, not the least of which is an *honest* husband—one who's a gentleman."

His jaw clenched. "I'm gentleman enough to leave you to sleep alone *tonight.*"

She shivered at his emphasis on *tonight.*

"But don't push me, or you'll make me forget my gentlemanly manners." A glance at the bed made his meaning clear.

Her stomach roiled. *I won't let him see my discomfort.* Prudence kept her shoulders straight and her chin up.

Briefly, Michael closed his eyes and shook his head. He sighed and opened his eyes. "You'll find a chamber pot under the bed."

His momentary weakness failed to soften her. "I suppose that's better than a journey outside to the outhouse in the dark."

Michael lifted his hand as if not knowing what to say, moved toward the crate, grasping the top slat with one hand and lifting. He turned to leave.

Prudence held out a hand in appeal. "Michael, are we really holding a party tomorrow? I like the idea of one, but I think you should postpone such an event until we have time to prepare."

He faced her. "I told my men there'd be a party, and I'm not going back on my word."

She let out a huff of annoyance.

"You've given parties before in St. Louis, haven't you?"

"Dinner parties. My mother was often ill and left me in charge."

"This is just a bunch of miners and a few of their wives. Probably *far* less work than a fancy dinner party. I'm sure you'll be fine."

"There's *far* more of your people. They won't all fit in the house. And there's no furniture on which to sit."

"They're used to standing."

"Mrs. Tisdale said there wasn't enough food to feed everyone," she argued, frustrated with his stubbornness.

"Of course there is. They'd be eating anyway." He held up a hand to forestall her response to such a ridiculous comment. "I'll send some men out hunting and fishing tomorrow. Take whatever you need from the store and the rooming house. I own both."

"That doesn't mean much." She crossed her arms in front of her chest. "I'm doing all the work for my own welcoming party. That's not right."

He shrugged. "The other women will help."

"I don't even know them," she protested.

"Then this event is a good way to become fast friends."

She remembered his prior mention of saloon girls. "I don't even know if they are the type of women with whom I want to associate."

His expression hardened. "Prudence, we have *nine* women in this tiny town, including the two saloon girls. You can't avoid associating with any of them, even Marla and Becky Lee. Those two do come out of the saloon to do shopping and such. Even if you crossed the street to avoid them, which I hope you won't, we're talking about a few feet of distance between you."

Prudence was too tired to think about the party and forming an acquaintance with nine women. She glanced at the tub. "My water is cooling."

"Well, good night, then." Michael turned and left the room.

Prudence waited until she heard the sound of his footsteps moving down the hall. With a sigh, she lifted her traveling coat from off the bedpost and threw the filthy garment into the corner. Then she walked to the door, pushed it closed, and turned the key in the lock. Leaning her forehead against the smooth wood, she fought the urge to burst into tears. *I won't give that man the satisfaction of making me cry, even if he'll never know.*

In spite of his body being almost limp with exhaustion, Michael couldn't fall asleep. His mind was too full of his new marriage, his difficult bride, the party, his wife's adjustment to the town, his people's reaction to her overt slight, and his doubts about Prudence's personality.

Earlier, he'd made several trips to the stables to bring back armfuls of straw to form a makeshift pallet on the floor of one of the bedrooms. He was thankful to avoid Howie, who lived in the stable. He didn't want the man catching a glimpse of his endeavors. After Prudence's inauspicious beginning in Morgan's Crossing, he didn't want to compound the gossip with rumors of them sleeping apart.

Michael had slept on the ground plenty of times, including the early days of owning the mine, which he'd won in a poker game. That first summer, he'd lived in a tent for months, laboring as hard as his men to scratch gold from the bowels of the earth. But lately, he'd become accustomed to a comfortable bed. *I've gotten soft.*

In the morning, Michael felt almost as tired as he had the night before. When he had fallen asleep, the problems with Prudence played out in his dreams. He tossed and turned on the lumpy pallet, and he awoke far too early, just as the first rays of daylight seeped through the uncurtained windows. All the ruminating about his situation hadn't solved a single problem, and he decided to head to the mine and forget about his wife for a while. *After a strong cup of coffee, of course.*

Michael made quick work of dressing, pulling clean clothing from the battered chest he'd moved from the big bedroom to this one last night. Then he went downstairs to wash up in the kitchen, not bothering to heat hot water to shave, figuring he could do so later before the party. *Prudence will just have to deal with a scruffy-looking husband today.* He bared his teeth in a feral grin and sauntered out the back door, heading for the boarding house along the path behind the buildings in search of coffee and breakfast.

This early, with the dark sky showing pink along the horizon, the town was still quiet. Soon, all the men without wives would converge on the dining room in the boarding house for breakfast. Sometimes, his China men joined them. But in the summer, the Orientals preferred to sleep for free in tents and prepare their own food rather than pay to live indoors.

Michael knew the path so well, he didn't need more light. Veering around a pothole he recalled lay under a tree branch arching over the track, he threaded through stacks of wooden crates, tossed haphazardly around the back yard of the boarding house, and entered through a door to the kitchen. The room was redolent with the smell of frying bacon and the bitter brew of coffee.

Cookie Gabellini, standing at the monster black stove, looked behind him. "Mornin', boss," he said, in a voice sounding of whiskey and smoke. An apron covered with several weeks' worth of food stains wrapped around his round middle. Like Michael, the man hadn't yet shaved. The cook only did so when Father Fredrick came to town and the man attended Sunday mass.

An Oriental boy, one of two who worked as helpers, nodded at Michael and carried a heavy pot with a ladle inside. He put his back against a set of swinging doors and disappeared into the dining room.

Oatmeal, Michael surmised, although sometimes the cook made beans in the morning. He moved around a rectangular table toward the stove, aiming for the big coffee pot. The soles of his boots crunched on the crumb-strewn floor.

"Didn't think I'd be seeing you here this morning," Cookie growled without looking up from the enormous frying pan of scrambled eggs he stirred with a wooden spoon. Strips of bacon sizzled in a frying pan. Deftly, he turned over several pieces with a fork. He grabbed a towel, stepped back, opened the door of the oven, and reached inside to pull out a tray of browned biscuits, which he set on a potholder on the table. He dropped the towel next to the tray.

Michael snatched a tin mug from a tottering stack and checked to make sure the inside was relatively clean. He snagged the towel from the table, wrapped the cloth around the handle of the coffee pot, and poured himself a cup.

Setting down the pot, he took a sip. The brew was hot and bitter, swirling with grounds, and right now, tasted like the nectar of the gods. Using the towel as protection, he scooped a biscuit from the tray, prying it open. The inside was almost as hard as the outside.

The other Oriental boy raced into the kitchen, pulled out a towel tucked in his waistband, grabbed the tray of biscuits, and hurried out, again using his back to push the door open.

Michael leaned over the stove, picked up the fork, and snagged two crisp strips of bacon, shoving them into the biscuit. He had a brief regretful thought of Mrs. Norton's light fluffy ones, dripping with butter and jam. But he was hungry enough to bite into his as soon as he judged the temperature cool enough, chewed, and swallowed. Belatedly, he recalled Cookie's question. "Mrs. Morgan is still sleeping, and I didn't want to disturb her. Need to head up to the mine."

Cookie shot him a knowing look, but had the decency to keep his mouth shut.

No, I did not wear out my wife with bedroom shenanigans. Michael figured he'd be getting plenty of knowing looks about something he *wasn't* getting any of. Glumly, he stared into his cup. *What in the heck am I goin' to do about Prudence?*

Perhaps if I act like a loving husband, I will feel more like one.

Chapter Thirteen

That morning, Prudence stood at the side of the bed, looking at the purple day dress she'd laid out, her throat tight. She'd had the shirtwaist and skirt made from material in her favorite color before she'd left St. Louis, with the idea of parading down the sidewalks of Morgan's Crossing wearing the dress, matching parasol shading her face. A hatbox, still in the trunk, held a lacy purple confection. She touched the lavender braid accenting the cuff of the sleeve. *Not today.*

So much for that daydream. The town doesn't even have sidewalks, only a dusty street.

At the agency, Mrs. Seymour had insisted Prudence purchase a work dress. Indeed, the matron had dragged her along to a store to select something practical and ready-made.

Prudence had stuffed the garment in the bottom of her second trunk, vowing never to wear the dreadful thing. *In the future, I'll have to be more careful of my vows.*

What are my choices? Go home? Pitch the biggest fit of my life at Michael for entrapping me? The idea appealed. She could vent the fear and anger boiling inside her since her arrival in Morgan's Crossing and her discovery of how completely the man had tricked her.

Normally Prudence wouldn't think twice about indulging in a

tantrum. She'd just explode. *But I'm trapped in the wilderness, far from civilization.* Common sense told her to wait and further assess the situation. *I can always get angry. I'm just postponing my eruption.* The idea pleased her, restoring a sense of control over a situation where earlier she'd felt so helpless.

The night before, Prudence had kicked her traveling dress and coat, as well as her undergarments, including the corset she'd worn, into the far corner. She studied the heap of fabric, not at all sure what to do with the articles of dirty apparel reeking with smoke, for they were beyond her laundry experience gained at the agency. Maybe the washerwoman could figure out how to clean them. *What was her name?*

Ah, Mrs. Rivera. After the day she'd had yesterday, Prudence was amazed she could remember the name of a servant she hadn't even met.

She glanced around the room. *I'm in desperate need of a wardrobe.* She wondered if the store in town carried furniture—even a piece she could use on a temporary basis. Downstairs, they needed a dining room table, too—perhaps a rough one that she could cover with one of her grandmother's linen tablecloths. She let out an exclamation of annoyance, realizing the barrel with her dishes and tablecloths was still in Sweetwater Springs.

Yes, checking out the store will be my first order of business.

Prudence dug through her trunk until she found the blue work dress. As much as she hated to make her first appearance in the garment, she had too much to do for the party tonight to worry about wearing nice clothing. She rummaged around in the trunk some more until she discovered an apron and tossed it on the bed. Both the dress and the apron were too wrinkled to wear without ironing. But she had neither iron nor board. *I'll have to speak to that woman about coming to iron every item in my trunks.*

But where will I hang everything? Prudence glanced around the room. Perhaps she could ask Michael or the stableman to rig up an indoor clothesline between the bedposts.

Straightening, Prudence dressed and brushed out her hair. Without a large mirror, she had to keep her hair simple, braiding the length into a plait and twisting the tail into a bun, stabbing hairpins to anchor the mass at the back of her head.

She picked up her silver hand mirror from the bed and examined herself, frowning at the plain hairstyle. Then she moved toward the fireplace, walking around the tub with the cold soapy water still inside. For want of a shelf, she laid the mirror on the mantel, next to the photo of Lissa in debutante white taken the year before she died. Prudence had more family photos in another trunk, but this one was her favorite, and she'd carried it in her satchel.

Dearest Lissa, if there are any strings you can pull for me up in heaven, I'm in sore need of your help. Prudence paused, not even sure what to ask for.

Before she could put her vague longings into words, Prudence heard the ringing of the bell outside the front doors. The thought of visitors made her heartbeat speed up. She glanced down at her work dress, wondering if she should hurriedly change, and tried to smooth out the wrinkles to no avail. *How embarrassing to appear before guests clad like this!*

She shrugged, trying to remember one of Mrs. Seymour's sayings about ladies, their inner fortitude and appearances. She couldn't quite remember the matron's advice. *I wish I hadn't tuned her out so often.* But her mother's wisdom came readily to mind, perhaps because Prudence had heard the reprimand on more occasions, or maybe because she'd repeated the words to herself only a few days prior. *You can always tell a lady by her air of good breeding—how she carries herself, the grace in her every gesture.*

Prudence hurried from the room and down the stairs. Through the glass in the doors, she could see two women standing inside the vestibule. When she drew closer, she recognized Mrs. Tisdale's snowy hair and moved to open the doors. "Good morning, ladies." She didn't usually sound so cheerful before breakfast, but she was pleased to have company.

"Glad to see you so chipper today, Mrs. Morgan. You'll excuse us, I know, for not dressing in our best clothes to make a proper call. With a party tonight, we have too much to do to indulge in frivolities."

Prudence gestured to her own clothing. "I'm of the same mind."

Mrs. Tisdale held up a covered plate. "I've brought breakfast. Hotcakes and sausage." She tilted her head to indicate the other woman. "And this here is Rosa, Mrs. Carlos Rivera, who often cleans and does Mr. Morgan's laundry."

Mrs. Rivera was as dark and spare as Mrs. Tisdale was white and plump. Their faded, worn dresses made Prudence's look like Sunday best. The older woman carried a plate covered with cheesecloth, and Mrs. Rivera had the handle of a basket over one arm, and a tin cup in the other hand.

Normally, Prudence would have barely given women like them the time of day. But remembering Michael's words of last night and seeing their friendly smiles made her open the door wider and wave them in.

Mrs. Tisdale walked into the study and set down the plate on the desk. She took off the cheesecloth and spread it out like a miniature tablecloth before picking up the plate and centering it on the cloth. "Mr. Morgan said to tell you he ate at the boarding house early this morning. He needed to get on up to the mine since he's been away for so long."

Prudence had a feeling her husband's early disappearance had more to do with avoiding her than with getting to his work.

Mrs. Rivera set the tin mug on the cloth. "We thought you'd prefer tea over coffee, but if we are wrong...?" Her soft voice held a slight Spanish accent.

"No, tea is fine."

Mrs. Rivera set the basket on the table and took out a setting of silverware, a napkin, a crock of butter and two jars of jam and one of honey. She tapped the lid of one of the jars. "We didn't know which you'd prefer on your hotcakes."

"Maple syrup, of course. But this morning I won't be picky."

"We've brought huckleberry and Saskatoon jam." Mrs. Rivera touched each jar to indicate which was which.

"So thoughtful of you. I've not tried either before, so I'll have to sample both."

Mrs. Tisdale put the finishing touches on the makeshift table, talking all the while. "Rosa and I have been conferring about the party. I think if all the women pitch in to help, we'll have this all worked out in two shakes of a lamb's tail."

Prudence wasn't familiar with that measurement of time, but hoped the woman didn't mean more than a few hours.

"I know for a fact that Mr. Morgan doesn't have dishes. He uses mine. So after the midday meal, we are going to borrow them from everyone in town, serving pieces as well, and bring them all here."

Prudence thought with longing of her grandmother's twenty-four piece table setting. *I should have left the second trunk and brought the crate.* "My husband said he'd send men to hunt and fish."

"He told us, and we've already sent word to the other women. And of course, they all want to contribute, so don't you worry about fixing dessert. Marla and Becky Lee won't bring food, of course, for they don't have access to a kitchen. They eat at the boarding house. But Becky Lee offered a tablecloth from her hope chest—"

"Hope chest," Prudence interrupted, astonished at the idea of a saloon girl having marriage in mind for her future. *Whoever would marry a fallen woman?* And Mrs. Tisdale and Mrs. Rivera sounded as if they actually associated with the two prostitutes.

Unimaginable. I certainly can't be expected to do likewise. She held in a *humph* of disapproval. *After the party, I'll have to raise the standards around here.*

The two women exchanged glances.

Uneasy, Prudence wondered if they'd discerned her thoughts. She needed the women too much today to alienate them.

Mrs. Tisdale sighed. "Although it pains me to say so, for it reflects as poorly on us as their choice of work does on Marla and Becky Lee...didn't the good Lord, Himself, associate with fallen women? To our shame, the ladies in Morgan's Crossing used to treat the saloon girls like dirt."

"We ignored them," Mrs. Rivera agreed.

"Then the winter before last, a sickness raced through town." She made a circling motion to encompass the whole place. "Caught nearly everyone and knocked them off their feet, Mr. Morgan included. Those unaffected, mostly the China men, for they had foreign herbs and such, nursed the sick ones. Well, our saloon girls pitched right in—caring for us as tenderly as if they were kin. The sickness eventually felled Becky Lee. Marla was the only woman who remained well, although run off her feet, she was, with so many to care for. She directed the men who hadn't succumbed as if she were a general ordering around her troops."

"We lost three adults and..." Mrs. Rivera looked down, her voice thickening. "Five children."

Mrs. Tisdale touched her friend's shoulder in a gesture of support. "Including Rosa's baby daughter. We would have lost far more without the help of those two women, and the China men, as well. Made me chagrined for being so judgmental. They might do wrong with..." she waved a hand in the direction of the saloon. "But the good book tells us not to judge others, so I think we were almost as sinful."

Prudence wasn't sure if she'd just been told a story or preached a sermon.

Mrs. Tisdale picked up the basket and set it on the floor. "We'll leave you to eat, Mrs. Morgan. Then, if you don't mind, bring back the dishes to my house. Don't bother to wash them."

Prudence hadn't intended to do so.

"Keep the jam and honey jars. My house is the second on the right just past the saloon. We can go check the pantry of the boarding house as well as the store for supplies for tonight."

"I'll only be a few minutes." She nodded a dismissal.

The two women smiled and saw themselves out.

As she sipped the tea, Prudence pondered those smiles— warm and genuine—the kind she'd seen many times directed at others. She wasn't used to having them shine at her, and the effect was oddly disconcerting, as if her normal world had turned upside down by such a simple action.

They are my servants, she tried to tell herself—to put the women in their proper sphere. But Mrs. Tisdale and Mrs. Rivera didn't seem to belong there, and Prudence couldn't quite bring herself to squash them into place.

She buttered her flapjacks and spread the first one with huckleberry jam. She cut a bite, and ate, enjoying the unusual taste. *Maybe I'll forego maple syrup, after all.*

Although Prudence told herself she should begin as she meant to go on—establish precedents from the beginning—another part of her realized she could wait. *I'm a newcomer and alone here. I'll bide my time.* She wasn't quite sure what to make of her circumspect behavior, but she knew the rest of her life could balance on these first few days.

Mrs. Seymour's words came back to her. *You'll find relationships with other women bring true comfort and support, something we are in dire need of at times.*

Perhaps the matron is right.

Wouldn't Mrs. Seymour be amused at how the strictures, which the woman must have thought bounced off of Prudence's brain—and, indeed, most had—now served as a guide in this unfamiliar territory?

She spread the second pancake with butter and tried the Saskatoon jam, finding the sweet, nutty taste equally delicious. *I can't choose which I like best.* Then Prudence realized she didn't have to. She could enjoy both in equal measure.

Maybe that's an analogy for my new life.

Only after Prudence had gone upstairs to put on a hat did she realize she still wore a wrinkled dress. With a sigh, she pulled out a small reticule. Tucked inside was a tiny card case containing the cards she'd so optimistically had printed in St. Louis. *Seems ridiculous to use them here.* But Prudence was determined to set an example and uphold proper standards. She took cotton gloves from her glove box and pulled them on, sliding the strings of the reticule over her wrist.

Lastly, she took a hatbox from the trunk, raised the lid, and lifted out her plainest straw hat with a blue grosgrain ribbon around the brim. Out of habit, Prudence glanced around for a mirror and then grimaced. *I must purchase one.* She set the hat on her head, jabbing in a hatpin, and walked from the room.

Downstairs, she stepped into the study to retrieve the basket with Mrs. Tisdale's dishes and walked outside for her first stroll through Morgan's Crossing. She slid the handle of the basket into the crook of her elbow. Disappointment stabbed her. *Wrinkled work dress, plain hat, and carrying dirty dishes. Not how I imagined my debut.*

Prudence stopped on the edge of the porch to look around her. To prolong having to face the reality of the mining town, she glanced up at the sky. The weather was fine, sunny and cooler than previous days, the sky stark and almost achingly blue with no hint of clouds. *How I wish the beauty overhead reflected down below.* She took a deep breath and prepared to study her new surroundings.

As she suspected, the bright light of day made the place look even more rag-tag. She bit her lip to hold in a groan. *Well, you've done it this time, Prudence Crawford,* she thought in a tone very like Mrs. Seymour's. *Prudence Morgan,* she hastily corrected, making a mental note to write to Mrs. Seymour just so she could use her new stationary and sign her name, *Mrs. Michael Morgan.*

Will being married be enough to make up for living here? Yesterday, flush with the excitement of Michael's attention, Prudence might have answered yes. But his rapid changes of mood disconcerted her. At times, he seemed to detest her, yet for the most part, he'd been perfectly polite.

With a shake of her head at the dilemma of her marriage, Prudence walked down the steps to the street. She lifted her skirt enough to keep the hem out of the dirt, wondering if she could persuade Michael to build sidewalks. Either that or wear her hems shorter. *Practical, but verging on scandalous.*

On the opposite side of the street, no building obscured the view of the dried grassland gradually sloping to the river and a bordering line of leafy trees. There was space between Michael's house, which was set back from the street and had big side yards, and neighboring log cabins. Curtains twitched as she passed the first one. *Someone must be watching.*

The two-story yellow boarding house came next, located across from the saloon, which was the first structure on the opposite side—a square unpainted box of a building with *Rigsby's Saloon* splashed in crooked letters over the door.

She shuddered and turned her face to the boarding house. A covered porch ran across the whole front of the clapboard building, with long benches on both sides of the door.

The store came next, looking far smaller than Prudence had expected. She frowned, doubting she'd find furniture in such an undersized place, and then crossed the street to the log house that must belong to Mrs. Tisdale.

Flowers bloomed in narrow beds in front of the house. She stepped onto the stoop and knocked.

The door opened, and Mrs. Tisdale beamed at her. "Welcome to my home, dear Mrs. Morgan."

The *dear* took Prudence aback. *First Mrs. Norton, and now Mrs. Tisdale.* Until she'd come to Montana Territory, she'd never been called *dear* in her life. She rather liked the experience.

"Let me take that." Mrs. Tisdale reached for the basket.

Prudence passed the basket, unfastened her reticle, and extracted her card case, which she opened. With a small flourish, she handed Mrs. Tisdale a card.

"What's this?" The woman squinted at the writing.

"My calling card," Prudence said with pride.

"Lovely. I like the roses on the border." The woman stepped back and gestured for Prudence to enter.

The cabin was dark with a low ceiling and only a small window by the door and one on the sidewall. A sheet hung across the corner, partly draped over a narrow bed. Under the curtained window was a second bed. A square table with four chairs, a small stove, and some boxes nailed on the walls for shelves completed the rest of the room. Prudence had never seen a house like this one and couldn't imagine living in such a cramped space. *Without privacy, the wintertime must be hellish.*

Mrs. Tisdale walked over to a box on the wall that seemed used for decoration, for a framed photograph of a young couple held pride of place in the middle alongside a blue glass box. She propped the card in front of the box, as if for display. "Pretty. I shall enjoy looking at it."

The compliment made her feel ashamed. Not that the woman was shaming her—far from it—but in comparison to this family, Prudence had *pretty* possessions in abundance. She'd been so busy complaining about how much she'd lost, she hadn't realized how much she still had. *I'm wealthy, indeed, in comparison to these people. I really need to feel grateful.*

Another one of Mrs. Seymour's precepts coming true.

Mrs. Tisdale donned her battered navy hat and tied on the ribbons. "Let's go get Rosa, shall we? And some of the other women will meet with us. Not Marla and Becky Lee, for they'll still be sleeping."

Prudence looked askance.

"They work until the late hours."

Thinking of what they did so late made heat rise in her face, and she stiffened.

"We only have one Oriental woman here—Jingy Guan, who arrived last summer to marry Hong Guan. Most of the older men are married, and they send money home to their wives. Hong arranged for his wife to sail to California and travel here. She doesn't speak a lick of English and keeps close to home."

She must be homesick.

"Julia Zaires and her baby are visiting family in Sweetwater Springs for the next few weeks, so you'll have to wait to meet her. Now Portia Rossmore, poor thing, isn't allowed out of the house to socialize without her husband."

"What?" Prudence exclaimed.

"Clyde Rossmore's a brute! And so I've told him to his face. And when I did, why that man clenched his fist and looked about to hit me. Probably would have, too, if my son hadn't been there." She rested her hands on her hips. "My Dean's mighty big, if I do say so myself."

Prudence swallowed, remembering Mrs. Seymour's warning about being smacked if she riled her husband. "Does he hit her?"

Mrs. Tisdale's lips pressed together, and sudden tears gleamed in her eyes. "I suspect Clyde took his rage with me out on the poor girl. The next day, I glimpsed bruises on her face, and I've felt guilty ever since. Portia is beautiful and sweet but frightened of her own shadow."

"Can't anyone do something?"

"Mr. Morgan has tried, and my Dean beat the tar out of that man when he once witnessed Clyde backhand Portia. He thought if Clyde knew how being hit felt, he'd stop." She shook her head. "No such luck."

Recalling that she was the first lady of this town, paltry as it was, Prudence had a sudden and unusual spurt of altruism. "She should leave him. We can help her."

"And where would she go? How would she support herself? Portia couldn't marry without a divorce, and Clyde would kill her when he caught up with her."

"There must be a way," Prudence said fiercely, astonished by her own reaction to a woman she hadn't met.

"Even if there were, Portia wouldn't leave him. I happen to know Mr. Morgan has offered."

A sudden unpleasant thought had Prudence narrowing her eyes.

Mrs. Tisdale held up her hand. "I see what you're thinking, but you're wrong. Mr. Morgan offered to send Portia to his family. Some of his brothers have farms. But she refused to leave. I can't imagine why."

Prudence couldn't either.

"Clyde might bring Portia to the party tonight, but he'll keep her at his side. A ball and chain, he is." Mrs. Tisdale straightened her hat. "Let's go meet the other ladies."

When they joined the three women clustered in front of the store, Mrs. Tisdale gestured. "Cecilia, Mrs. Leviticus Garr. Ava, Mrs. Paulo Tuccio, and Verna, Mrs. George Copelin."

"Mrs. Morgan," they murmured, dipping their chins.

Like Mrs. Tisdale and Rosa Rivera, the three wore faded work dresses and old straw hats, although Ava had woven a wreath of fresh flowers around the brim of hers.

"I'm afraid our store doesn't have much to offer, Mrs. Morgan," Ava said with a shake of her head that sent a daisy flying to land in the dirt.

Not unlike my traveling hat.

Verna Copelin, tall and thin, with wiry ginger hair and a narrow, freckled face, gave a longsuffering sigh. "In fact, we'd be obliged if you could encourage Mr. Morgan to expand the offerings," she uttered in plaintive tones.

Prudence frowned at this confirmation of her fears. "I'd heard that a mercantile is usually the center of activity in a small town."

"Not ours," Ava Tuccio said in tone of disgust. "How I miss shopping, stopping in a cafe for afternoon tea…"

Ava's olive skin, dark hair and eyes, and Italian accent reminded Prudence of Lina Barrett, giving her an immediate dislike of the woman—although she had enough presence of mind not to show it.

Cecilia Garr, plump and pretty, with a heart-shaped face and blue eyes, tossed her head and bounced the blonde tendrils framing her face. "As you see, Mrs. Morgan, we are in sore need of a woman who has the power to take charge in this town."

Although the woman spoke with the thickest Southern accent Prudence had ever heard, the words made her glow with a feeling of self-importance. She bestowed an approving smile on Mrs. Garr. "My sentiments exactly!"

Mrs. Copelin shook her head. "I doubt you'll be able to accomplish much. This is a mining town, after all. The needs of a few women and children don't count."

Dread grew in Prudence. "How about I see for myself?" She marched up to the store.

The women followed like a gaggle of geese.

On both sides of the door, the two big windows were so dirty Prudence couldn't see through them. Her eagerness to look inside vanished. *What kind of store doesn't display goods for sale?* A glance behind her to the women and the poor excuse for a town gave her an answer—*one that has captive customers.*

This isn't right! For all that people had no choice in shopping here, the store should still look appealing, should invite people in to do business.

Taking a breath in preparation, she opened the door and strode inside, inhaling the smell of coffee beans, leather, and dust. The filthy windows made the interior light dim despite the presence of another small window near the back counter. Prudence glanced around in growing dismay, seeing a whole wall of men's clothing and boots, plenty of tools, barrels that must hold flour, beans, and other foodstuffs, but little to satisfy a woman's needs.

Slowly, she circled the perimeter. She had to search before finding three thin bolts of fabric, recognizing the middle one from the curtains in Mrs. Tisdale's house and the skirt Mrs. Copelin wore, while Mrs. Garr's green dress was made from the cloth of the bottom bolt.

Some shelves held jars of jam, pickles, and honey. Prudence walked closer and saw a solitary tin of tea. Leaning for a closer look, she gasped at the outrageous price. She pivoted to double check the room, not glimpsing a single item she'd want to purchase.

Her stomach tight, she walked over to view the label on the shelf holding the bolts of fabric. The outrageous charge for cloth that Prudence would only use for rags was almost as costly as finer material in St. Louis.

The door opened, and the women silently filed in, fitting themselves around boxes and barrels.

Prudence could only stare at them speechless.

They watched her for a long moment.

Prudence spread out her hands in a helpless gesture, finally finding words. "Is this the only place you can shop?" She glanced at Mrs. Copelin's skirt. "For material and other garments?"

Mrs. Copelin's expression pinched. "Mr. Hugely says he won't order more fabric until these bolts are used up."

"I've never heard of such a thing!" Prudence exclaimed. "But what if you need...say, a hat?"

"We tell Mr. Hugely what we need, and he places an order. Quite expensive that is, though, so we usually make do with what we already have."

"What about placing your own order through the Montgomery Ward catalogue?"

They gave her blank stares.

Mrs. Tisdale shook her head. "I don't know what that is."

Unheard of. Prudence gave a helpless glance around the room. "How do you manage?"

Mrs. Tisdale's mouth pulled to one side. "We barter. I knit socks, caps, scarves, and mittens. Mrs. Copelin keeps chickens, and we get eggs from her. Mrs. Tuccio has a cow. Mrs. Garr makes soap for laundry and bathing, the China men raise pigs...."

"I see." Prudence looked toward the counter and arched an eyebrow. "Where is Mr. Hugely?"

"No doubt he's at the river with a pole in his hands, using the excuse that the boss ordered the men to fish and hunt."

Mrs. Tuccio placed her hands on her hips. "Or napping in his chair on the back porch."

Prudence couldn't believe her ears. *This no way to run a business.* "And he just left the store open? What about thieves?"

Mrs. Garr shrugged. "Well, someone might steal some candy and eat it quick. Otherwise, everything is recognizable."

"Let's go see if he's napping. Lead me to him."

Mrs. Tisdale tilted her head toward a door behind the counter. "Doubt we want to go through his bedroom to get out the back. Let's use the front door."

The ladies trooped out and around the building. On a small open porch, shaded by a tree, a fat man slept in a worn leather chair. His head lolled, and he snorted a snore.

Prudence stepped up on the porch.

The ladies stayed on the ground behind her.

"Mr. Hugely," Mrs. Tisdale said in a strident tone.

The man shook himself awake and stared at the gathered group, his thin white hair sticking out. Seeing Prudence, he pushed his way out of his chair. "No need to introduce yourself," he said in the jovial tone of a snake oil salesman. "You're Mrs. Morgan. Delighted to meet you. How may I be of service?"

She ignored his attitude. "I was just perusing your store, Mr. Hugely. I found myself wondering at the high prices."

"Ah, shipping charges, my dear lady. You have no idea how much hauling goods from the railroad to Morgan's Crossing costs."

Perhaps the man is correct. "And the lack of variety for the women?"

"Don't have much call for feminine gew-gaws, Mrs. Morgan. If any of the women need anything, all they have to do is place an order with me." He raised his hands, palms up, in a helpless gesture. "Oh, course, those pesky shipping charges still apply."

"I see." Prudence made a mental note to investigate the *pesky* shipping charges. "We'll be back in a short while to gather supplies for the party."

"I'll see you later, then." The man's congenial tone didn't match his hard blue eyes.

"Indeed, you will." Prudence turned to leave. But before she walked down the steps, she looked over her shoulder. "Oh, and Mr. Hugely…wash those windows. I want to see them sparkling when I return."

Without waiting to see his reaction, Prudence stepped off the porch, knowing the man was probably shooting daggers at her back. But the glee on the faces of the women sustained her. "Now, ladies, we must head to the boarding house to take stock. If the store is anything to go by, I shudder to think of the state that place is in."

Chapter Fourteen

As the day faded to night, Prudence prepared for the party by donning a favorite teal silk gown, newly pressed by Mrs. Rivera, who'd also helped coif her hair. In the kitchen, with judicious use of the curling iron heated on the stove and a great many hairpins, the woman created a soft style, which—at least from the small view in her hand mirror—enhanced Prudence's plain features. Mrs. Rivera had also helped Mrs. Tisdale empty the bathtub and lug it downstairs to store on the back porch before the two women returned home.

In her bedroom, dressing by touch made Prudence realize how much she'd always depended on seeing herself in a large mirror. *At least at the agency, I learned to do without a maid. I can hardly call upon my neighbors when I need help getting dressed.*

I have a husband now. The thought of Michael tightening her corset strings…or *loosening* them made her stomach quiver. *No, I'm certainly not ready for his help.*

She straightened the ruffles around the low-cut neck of the gown, which added fullness to her meager bustline, and puffed the short sleeves. The back of the dress draped in a slide of ruffles over the full bustle.

Prudence hadn't worn the dress since before her father'

death, and then she'd gone into mourning, so the gown was slightly out of style—not that anyone here could tell. Technically, she was still in mourning for her mother, but no one knew that fact. She hated wearing black, for the color washed out her complexion, and she'd discarded her mourning garb as soon as she'd arrived at the agency, stuffing the dresses into the bottom of trunk number three.

Prudence centered a green jade heart in the hollow of her throat—a necklace that had once belonged to Lissa—given to her sister by their father who'd had business dealings in the Orient. Wearing the necklace made her feel close to Lissa. *Give me courage tonight, dear sister.* She dabbed floral scent on her wrists and behind her ears. Finally, she drew on her long gloves.

With a swish of silk, she left the bedroom. At the staircase, Prudence hesitated, resting her hand on the banister. She looked down to see Michael waiting at the foot of the staircase.

The dusky light from the windows cast him into shadows. He'd shoved one hand into the pocket of the same suit he'd worn for their wedding. The other held the curved newel post. His head was bent, as if staring at his feet.

For the first time, Prudence wondered how her husband really felt about this party, if he struggled with this marriage as much as she did. *Doubts and delights, one after another, with the doubts winning.*

She placed a gloved hand on the railing and with her other gathered up a fold of her skirt, just enough to keep her feet from tangling in the hem and disrupting her entrance. She descended slowly, her carriage regal.

At the sound of her heels on the stairs, Michael looked up and straightened, his eyes widening and lips curving. "Well, well." He placed a foot on the first step and held out a hand to lead her down the rest of the way. "You will dazzle everyone tonight, my dear Pru. A fitting first lady."

Heat from his compliment swirled in her stomach, up her chest, and into her cheeks, making Prudence feel pretty and confident.

When she stepped onto the floor, Michael brought her hand to his lips. He stared into her eyes for a moment. "You have witchy eyes, my Pru, the way they change. Tonight, you are a sea nymph."

She cast him a look of doubt, but his gaze seemed sincere, and she savored his compliment.

Michael turned to wave at the borrowed chairs lining the hallway. "I'm most impressed with all you've managed to accomplish today." Holding her hand, he guided her to the doorway of the dining room, where the rich smell of roasted meat, baked fish, and other foods mingled in the air.

Prudence thought the fireplace—surrounded by small squares of royal-blue tile, with a full mantelpiece comprised of several shelves—was the best part of the dining room. She imagined displaying some of her grandmother's blue-and-white china, those pieces and the tiles complimenting each other.

Even though Prudence surveyed the dining room with critical eyes, imagining how her acquaintances in St. Louis might scoff, she couldn't help feeling some pride in what she and the other women had scrounged together for this makeshift party.

I certainly can't fault their enthusiasm.

Becky Lee's white linen tablecloth covered two borrowed tables pushed together to form one long surface with uneven sides. Mrs. Copelin's silver candlesticks, polished to a shine, held white candles, as yet unlit. Cheesecloth-covered bowls and platters of food—rabbit, squirrel, and fish from today's hunting efforts, venison from a buck brought down a few days ago by Howie, a small roasted pig donated by the China men, and other dishes prepared by the women—took up most of the improvised table.

In one corner sat a stack of tin, enamel, and china plates, with utensils in a basket next to them. Borrowed napkins in all colors—some, in Prudence's opinion, little more than rags—were neatly piled on the other side of the plates.

Through the window, she could see into the backyard—plain dirt shaded by trees with a stable on the far end. The tables and benches from the dining room of the boarding house were placed under the trees—scrubbed first, of course. Each held lanterns taken from the mine. Prudence doubted a light remained anywhere else in town. *Good thing the moon is almost full tonight.*

Michael released her hand. "Let me light the candles." He moved to the table.

Prudence waved to the oil lamp on the mantelpiece. "Those as well. With borrowing so many, we should have plenty of light."

While Michael lit the candles and the lamps, Prudence peeked into the kitchen, inhaling the scent of cinnamon and vanilla. The mammoth black stove dominated the big room, but the space lacked other necessary furniture. A built-in counter along one wall with cupboards above and below accommodated a line of pies, cakes, and plates of cookies, as well as another stack of small tin plates.

Prudence had never seen so many different desserts in one place. Looking at the abundance of treats, she hoped there'd be enough to satisfy everyone's sweet tooth. She suspected the miners wouldn't confine themselves to dainty servings, as did polite guests at fancy parties in St. Louis. *Although this is as far from a fancy party as can be.*

One of the saloon women had sent by way of Mrs. Tisdale the Mason jar with wildflowers that sat at the far end of the counter. Prudence noted another platter of cookies that hadn't been there before and shook her head in amazement. *In the last half hour, one of the women must have slipped into the house through the back door while I was upstairs dressing.*

Throughout the day, the women of Morgan's Crossing—except for the two saloon girls, Jingy Guan, and Portia Rossmore—had gleefully labored for this party, displaying a liveliness that Prudence found infectious. *Why, if I'd worked so hard at the agency, I would have felt grumpy, not cheerful. Everyone around me would have known of my dissatisfaction.*

Truth be told, because of the way the others deferred to her, the laughter and the stories, Prudence hadn't minded the work.

She'd never realized the difference congenial companions made, although at the agency she'd seen the other brides enjoy the benefits of similar friendships. Darcy and Kathryn had particularly relished doing the household chores together. Like Prudence, those two had come from an upper-class background and been equally ignorant of domestic matters. They'd encouraged each other and laughed at their mistakes, while Prudence only fumed at hers.

A small regret stabbed her. *Maybe things could have been different with us if I'd joined in, instead of....*

Michael joined her in the doorway, slipping an arm around her waist.

The unexpected intimacy startled her, and she stiffened.

He started to pull away, but Prudence stopped him by leaning against his side. She had to tilt her head back so he could see her face. So near, she could smell the bay rum soap he'd used, the masculine scent as intimate as their closeness. "Do you think there will be enough food?" she asked. "I have no way of judging."

"Nope," he said with a grin.

Prudence straightened, staring at him in dismay.

He tapped her nose. "Don't look so concerned, my dear. My men are like locusts. They'll chomp down the food until none remains. I doubt even crumbs will be left."

"That isn't amusing, Michael. What are we to do if we run out?" *No good hostess in St. Louis would bear the shame.*

"I didn't mean to distress you, Pru. Parties are rare in Morgan's Crossing, so everyone will enjoy themselves, regardless. You'll see. People here are used to eating up all the food, leaving none left over."

Pru. Usually she hated anyone chopping her name in half. But the way Michael's voice caressed the word each time he used the nickname gave *Pru* a new and special meaning.

"I have a surprise for you."

Her heart gave a little leap. Surprises had seldom come her way. "What?"

Michael tilted his head toward the front door. "Come see." He took her hand again.

They walked through the entry, passing the parlor where the ladies had pushed the settee against the back wall and the leather chair into a corner. Wooden chairs borrowed from the neighbors and the boarding house lined the sides.

Prudence barely noticed the sparse décor, focusing more on the feel of her husband's hand clasping hers. In the last few minutes, he'd touched her more than anyone had in years. *Cumulatively.*

With sudden sadness, Prudence realized she hadn't even known she'd lacked physical affection. *I took my parents' aloofness for granted.*

Michael held open one of the inner doors for her. She crossed the vestibule, and he pushed aside the outer doors. Together, they stepped out onto the porch.

From each corner of the roof hung a round, red-silk sphere with a glow inside. "Oh! Whatever are those?" Prudence released Michael's hand and moved closer to examine one, admiring the golden patterns painted on the silk. "I've never seen the like. They cast such a pretty light."

"Jingy Guan brought them with her when she came from China. I've borrowed them for tonight."

"How wonderful." Prudence whirled and walked back to him. She looked up into his handsome face, feeling in more charity toward her husband than she had since her arrival. "Thank you, Michael. They are a unique, festive touch." She placed a hand on his arm and squeezed.

His gaze grew intense. He trailed a finger up the side of her neck and under her chin.

She shivered, catching her breath on an exquisite sense of excitement.

Michael's finger paused under her chin. He bent his head, and his mouth closed over hers.

With a small sigh, Prudence parted her lips, bringing her hand up and flattening her palm on his chest where his heart beat strongly. The touch of his mouth on hers sent a quiver through her body. *So this is how a kiss feels—the heat, the softness, the manliness....* Dizzy with sensation she wanted more.

At the sound of voices, Michael lifted his head. But he kept his gaze on her face for a lingering moment before stepping back and releasing her.

Prudence pulled away, her cheeks heating, still feeling the possession of his lips on hers. She hoped the dimming light hid her telltale color.

A girl about eight years old or so ran up to the house, followed by a boy who looked a couple years younger and another boy about the same age as the girl. All three had eager smiles.

Prudence didn't think they were siblings, for the youngest boy was redheaded, green-eyed, and freckle-faced, the girl had dark hair and eyes and olive skin, and the older boy had thick brown hair in a bowl cut and curious blue eyes.

The children bounded up the steps and over to them.

"Mr. Morgan," said the girl, who bore a strong resemblance to Rosa Rivera. She spread her skirt to show the tiny red flowers on the blue material. "I'm wearing my new dress. I'm supposed to save it for Sundays when Father Fredrick says Mass. But Mamá said parties are special times."

"Your mama is right. And quite pretty you look, too, Juanita." He smiled at the redheaded boy. "I'll bet you're hungry, Rufus."

"Sure am." His grin showed a missing tooth.

"Bobby," he said to the older boy, "did your grandma introduce you to Mrs. Morgan?"

"No, sir." The older boy flashed Prudence an impudent grin. "Ain't seen Miz Morgan, yet. Robert Tisdale, ma'am, at your service." He dipped a little bow.

Juanita whirled to face Prudence, her black braids swinging out. She took in the teal-blue dress, and her eyes widened in obvious awe.

Astonished at the sudden appearance of the children,

Prudence stared from the three to Michael. She hadn't seen any children all day and only now realized the lack. Nor had she seen a school or met a teacher, and she made a mental note to investigate the educational status of the town. She leaned close to him. "What are they doing here?"

Michael gave her a quick warning glance. "A party in Morgan's Crossing means *everyone*, even babes in arms."

"But whatever are we to do with them?"

"They'll entertain themselves. They usually do."

Prudence had no time to say anything more, for the children's families followed them up the steps, crowding onto the porch.

Mrs. Tisdale strode alongside a boulder of a man—her son Dean, judging from his resemblance to her and Bobby. She wore a navy-blue dress of finer material than her working one, yet still as simple in cut.

But her good-natured expression makes up for the deficits of her apparel. Prudence stumbled over the oddly protective thought.

Smiling a gap-toothed grin, Mrs. Tisdale waved a finger at Prudence. "Now, Mrs. Morgan, you are to enjoy your party. Just leave all the doings to us."

Prudence laughed. "Gladly."

Next came Rosa Rivera, her hand tucked in the crook of her husband's arm, followed by more families. After quick introductions, the men and children went into the house. The women lingered.

Mrs. Rivera gazed at the teal gown, pressing a hand to her cheek. "I ironed that dress but to see you wearing it, *ah…*"

"Thank you," Prudence said, pleased at the sincerity of the comment.

Mrs. Garr stopped and dramatically placed a hand on her chest, staring at Prudence's dress. She wore a pretty gown in sky blue, the straight skirt showing an out-of-date style, and held the hand of a small girl, who had the same heart-shaped face and curly blonde hair as her mother. "Why, that's such a beautiful gown, Mrs. Morgan," her Southern accent a thick coating on her words. "Mah sister sent me a magazine page she'd cut out. The picture is of a dress like yours." She sighed and tugged at her skirt. "This has been mah best dress since before mah marriage. I don't dare gain another pound, for the seams are completely let out."

Prudence preened at their compliments, enjoying being the center of attention. *This is more like what I imagined.*

None of the women wore bustles—even small padded ones. She shifted so they could view the silhouette of her gown, with the fabric draped over the bustle.

Dour Verna Copelin joined Prudence and the three other women.

All of them here to celebrate me! How very pleasant the event is turning out. Prudence glanced at Michael.

Her husband smiled, standing back to let the women gather around her.

Mrs. Copelin wore her wiry reddish hair slicked back into a tight bun so that no tendrils dared escape. She sniffed, sending a pointed glance at Prudence's bustle. "Can't see how you can move in that contraption. Certainly can't sit comfortably." But her eyes held obvious envy.

Prudence ignored the implied slight, glancing at Mrs. Garr's small daughter. "Where were the children today?"

Mrs. Tisdale looked at Mrs. Rivera. "We wanted them out from underfoot. So Juanita and Bobby watched them at the Garr's house. Juanita is good with little ones, and Bobby keeps them corralled and entertained."

"My boys helped catch fish," Mrs. Copelin said, a proud smile altering her customary severe appearance and making her freckled face look impishly pretty.

Taken aback by the change of countenance, Prudence couldn't help but wonder which expression was the true manifestation of the woman's spirit. *Had Verna once been a blithe girl? If so, what had made her change?* The thought made her uncomfortable, and she turned her attention back to the conversation. "I supposed school isn't in session yet?"

Mrs. Tisdale exchanged a glance with the other women, and then shook her head. "We have no school."

"What?" Prudence looked askance at Michael. "How can that be?"

He held up a hand to quell the conversation. "We'll talk about this later."

"We certainly will." Prudence added the topic to her growing list.

With an expansive gesture, Michael waved to those lingering on the porch. "Go on in."

Earlier in the day, when she'd thought of this evening, Prudence had assumed she and Michael would stand in a receiving line in the entryway of the house, while he introduced her to the townsfolk. But they never had a chance to move from the porch, for what seemed like an unending stream of men filed past them.

Most of the miners had obviously slicked themselves up, for their hair was neat, faces scrubbed, clothes clean, although Prudence saw patches and wrinkles a plenty, and a few straw or faded bowler hats carried in work-hardened hands.

Michael made introductions.

Prudence nodded and smiled, not even bothering to try to remember names unless someone stood out from the rest. She barely acknowledged Cookie Gabellini, who ran the boarding house. The state of his kitchen and dining room had so disgusted her that she hadn't remained in the building for more than the few minutes necessary to ascertain what supplies, place settings, and furniture were available. The boarding house was another project on her list. She couldn't allow her husband's miners to live in that hovel.

Mr. Hugely was the only man besides Michael who wore a suit, although in contrast to Michael's well-cut apparel, the shopkeeper's cheap red waistcoat strained across his stomach. "How lovely you are tonight, Mrs. Morgan," he said, his tone effusive. "You shine on us with your presence."

Prudence ignored the false praise. She knew better than to listen to a snake-oil salesman, especially one who she'd made wash windows.

With happy squeals, two women rushed up the porch steps.

From their shorter skirts and the paint on their faces, Prudence had no problem distinguishing the saloon girls. Even as her back started to stiffen at meeting them, she reminded herself that Becky Lee had given Mrs. Tisdale the tablecloth from her hope chest, and Marla had collected the bouquet of wildflowers. She couldn't cut their acquaintance when they'd contributed to the party, but she didn't have to warmly welcome them either.

In the darkening night, the China men appeared together in a silent group. Most looked to have wiry builds and wore their slick, dark hair in tails down their back. They gave her respectful nods and short bows but didn't speak.

A man and a woman several inches shorter than Prudence stopped in front of her, nodding and smiling.

"Hong Guan and his wife, Jingy," Michael said, waving toward a hanging red lantern. "These are from her."

"Jing-*Wei*." Hong accented the second syllable, as if sending a message about his wife's name. "She speakee no English."

I thought her name was Jingy? "Jing-Wei?" Prudence repeated to make sure.

Michael lifted his eyebrow. "Jing-Wei," he murmured to correct his error.

Jing-Wei, short and sturdy, bobbed her head and smiled. She was dressed in a black silk tunic and loose-fitting trousers. The odd garment looked comfortable.

"Thank you for loaning us your lanterns." Prudence waited while Hong translated. *If this town is such a shock to me, what must living here be like to someone from the Orient?* She couldn't even imagine traveling from a foreign land to a town with no other women of her kind, and not even understanding the language. *Perhaps we can teach her English.*

Jing-Wei touched her throat and pointed toward Prudence's necklace. She murmured something in Chinese.

Her husband nodded. "She say, bring good luck. Mean the jade."

"Oh, how nice to know." *I need all the luck I can get.* Filled with warmth from the good will everyone had directed her way, Prudence dared to hope her luck was already changing.

Finally, the stream of people ended.

Once the last man disappeared inside, Prudence let out a relieved breath. "Our house must be filled to the rafters."

Michael chuckled. "Oh, no, my dear. Only the first floor of the house is packed to the gills. There's no light upstairs, so no one will be on the second floor." He glanced down the road, his brows drawn together.

"What?" she asked, following his gaze.

"The Rossmores haven't come. And where in the heck is Obadiah Kettering?"

"Who is Obadiah Kettering?"

"Our entertainment."

She made a sound of exasperation. "That's not an answer."

Smiling, Michael winked. "You just wait." Placing a hand under her elbow, he guided her inside.

That wink made something curl deep within her that she didn't have time to examine. Indoors, as Prudence expected, the men took up most of the available space, even spilling up the staircase. They'd left a narrow path through the entryway just wide enough for Michael and Prudence to walk through.

With all eyes on her, she moved with her most regal air, bestowing nods and slight smiles on the populace, reveling in being the center of attention. For these few minutes, she didn't mind that her audience consisted only of a bunch of rough miners and their wives.

Michael paused by the entrance to the dining room, where Mrs. Tisdale and her formidable son stood guard, and turned Prudence so they faced everyone. He placed a hand on the small of her back. "My dear guests. Thank you for gathering to welcome my wife. Morgan's Crossing has long been in need of a first lady, and now we have one. I predict Mrs. Morgan will initiate some much needed changes."

Is the enthusiasm in his voice real? She gazed over the sea of faces, noting the ones she recognized. Some looked wary, some impassive, but most appeared welcoming, as if they were willing to give her a second chance after last night's blunder regarding the unwashed stink of the men. A strange sensation niggled in her stomach, one she couldn't identify.

Before Prudence could figure out the feeling, she saw the men near the door step aside, opening a space to reveal a man and a woman.

The blonde woman was heavy with pregnancy. Her tightly pulled-back hair and plain gray dress belied her delicate beauty. After a brief glance at Prudence, she kept her gaze lowered. Her shadowed blue eyes didn't make contact with anyone.

Portia Rossmore. The tragic figure stirred Prudence's pity, a rare occurrence.

The man Mrs. Tisdale called a brute stood with his hand around his wife's arm in an obvious too-tight grasp.

From the description she'd heard, Prudence had expected a big beast of a man, one more Dean Tisdale's size, instead of one of middling height.

At first glance, Clyde Rossmore seemed ordinary enough. He wore his brown hair slicked back, and a round-cut beard hid his chin. Like the clothing of most of the men, his shirt and pants were well worn but clean, and with no jacket in sight. His apparel was pressed to stiffness, attributed, no doubt, to his cowed wife. He caught Prudence's stare, and his light gray eyes narrowed.

Nothing in the look indicated intimidation, but nevertheless a frisson shivered down her spine. She wanted to step closer to Michael but gathered her courage and held her ground, her chin lifted.

Michael paused in his speech, shifting closer to Prudence as if in protection.

The couple slowly approached them.

"Clyde." Michael's tone wasn't welcoming. "Portia."

Prudence wondered at his use of their given names.

"I'd like you to meet my wife, Mrs. Morgan."

Prudence inclined her head toward Clyde, and then ignored him to give Portia a warm smile. "I'm delighted you could attend our party."

The woman's gaze skittered away.

"We wouldn't miss this shindig for the world," Clyde boomed, his false bonhomie sounding more brutish than his appearance suggested.

Prudence glanced up at Michael.

His gaze went beyond the Rossmores to sweep around the room. "Normally as good hosts—" He raised his voice to address the crowd. "—We'd allow you all to attack the food first. But since I've already warned my wife how nothing will be left after the ravening horde sweeps through—"

Laughter rumbled through the room.

Michael's smile widened. "And since this is a party in honor of my new bride, she and I will be the first to avail ourselves of the choice delicacies prepared by the lovely ladies of our town." He started to guide her into the dining room when applause broke out, and he halted, grinning and nodding in acknowledgment.

As Prudence glanced around, she saw smiles of genuine delight—whether because of the party or her presence or the thought of the feast to come. *Maybe all three.* She tried to keep a cynical grasp on her emotions, but as the clapping swelled into a crescendo, she gave herself up to the moment. *I could never have imagined I'd enjoy a gathering like this!*

"Kiss, kiss!" a man called out from the back of the room.

Other voices joined. "Kiss her!"

"Give her a kiss, boss!"

Prudence's cheeks heated. She glanced around but there was nowhere to retreat, so she gave in with good grace, lifting her face to his.

Laughter in his eyes, Michael lightly bussed her on the lips.

"Come on, boss, you can do better than that," another man yelled.

The voice sounded familiar, but she didn't look around to see who the instigator might be.

Holding his hand up for quiet, Michael laughed. "Perhaps I can. But not in front of witnesses. And I'm sure you all must be as famished as I am and, thus, anxious to do justice to the feast prepared by our dear ladies."

When she felt Michael signal with the pressure of his hand on her back, Prudence walked past the sentinel Tisdales and into the dining room. Someone, probably Mrs. Tisdale, had removed the cheesecloth from all the dishes.

"Ah," Michael half-said, half-sighed. "A feast for a bride—venison, pork, and fresh-caught trout. I believe I see six types of beans, creamed corn, and mashed potatoes. I recognize Cookie's biscuits by how brown they are."

Prudence laughed. "Michael, stop cataloguing the food, else your ravening horde will overwhelm us, and we'll end up with nothing to eat."

"You're right." He chuckled and handed her a china plate. "After you, my dear."

After only a second's debate about keeping her portions to a ladylike size, Prudence moved around the table, serving herself a sampling of this and a bit of that. Her portions remained a proper size, but the food piled high on her plate. When she finished the circuit, she stopped to wait for her husband.

Likewise, Michael held an overflowing plate. "Best to try everything, so as not to cause offence."

"Oh, is that your excuse?" she said archly.

"Absolutely, my wife." With his chin, he indicated the kitchen door. "I believe we have a special place reserved for us outside."

We do? Prudence had supervised the setting up of the tables and chairs in the back yard; she didn't recall anything special about their placement. But when she stepped outside, she saw another of the Chinese lanterns shedding a pink glow over a small square table, covered by a white cloth. In the middle, a glass vase held white roses.

The scene was quite romantic, and something in her heart

stirred. "Where did all this come from? And the roses? I didn't see any blooming around here." Flowers had been scarce in her brief tour of plain, dusty Morgan's Crossing.

Michael grinned. "The table is from my office at the mine. The tablecloth is from Becky Lee's hope chest. The vase is Mrs. Garr's prized possession, and Mrs. Tisdale brought the roses. She has a bush in her back garden."

"Oh, how thoughtful of you." Prudence blinked back sudden tears, surprised by a silly wave of emotion.

Michael's expression softened.

Is that tenderness I see? She desperately hoped so—longed for this evening to be real, not just a manipulation on her husband's part to win his workers' acceptance of her, as well as her capitulation to his bed. *And thus to woo me into remaining in this poky mining town.*

But, for the first time, the idea of living in Morgan's Crossing held merit.

Originally, Michael had issued the party invitation out of anger with his wife's behavior. All day long, he'd told himself he'd act like a besotted groom at the party, even if he didn't feel like one, and made arrangements to add some romantic touches to the evening, hoping to please Prudence enough so they could begin the physical side of their marriage.

But tonight, he found himself in unexpected harmony with her. When Prudence walked down the stairs—a shimmering vision in blue-green and the very sea nymph he'd named her—she'd poleaxed him, for he'd firmly fixed in his mind the idea of his mail-order bride as a plain woman, a female broodmare who'd warm his bed, wash his clothes, cook his meals, and take over the supervision of womanly enterprises in his town. *Maybe my resolve to act more loving to my wife won't be so difficult after all.*

Prudence still wasn't pretty, but she certainly had an elegant style that he admired. The looser hairstyle softened her features, and the color of her dress turned her eyes blue-green. *Dream eyes.* He wondered how they'd look filled with passion. *If I play my cards right, maybe I'll find out tonight.* The thought sent a surge of excitement through his body.

After they'd eaten, he'd turned her loose on the townsfolk, not sure what to expect of her behavior—the haughtiness she'd sometimes shown since her arrival, or the friendly manners he'd seen tonight when Prudence interacted with the other women. As he made his social rounds, Michael kept an eye on his bride, sometimes drifting to her side for a while, and then sliding away when she began talking with one of the women and the topic became too feminine.

He was just about to send his stableman, Howie, in search of Obadiah Kettering, when the fiddler staggered through the door, violin in hand. Michael let out a sigh of relief, which turned into a frown when he saw the man's inebriated condition. He'd given orders to close the saloon early, but Obadiah could still have imbibed from a bottle he'd stashed away.

The musician was stick-thin, with long spidery legs and arms that belied his ability to swing a pick. He'd changed clothes, but judging from the stench, hadn't bothered to bathe. "Howdy, boss." He slurred his words, swaying in place.

Michael clamped down a surge of anger. *Drunk or stone-cold sober, the man can play a fine tune, and that's all that matters tonight.* He leaned forward. "You're lucky I don't have you tossed in the river to sober up," he growled, keeping his voice low, leaving the man in no doubt of his displeasure. "Clean you up, too."

Obadiah opened his mouth to retort.

Quickly regretting his close proximity to the fiddler, Michael shook his head in warning, stepping out of smelling range. "You remember the first song I want you to start with?"

"Yah, Boss. 'Skater's Waltz' by Waldteufel." He gave a mournful shake of his head. "Won't be the same without an orchestra."

"As you've already told me ten times." Earlier today, Michael had wasted half a frustrating hour going over musical selections with the man. He wanted something classy for his first dance with Prudence. He jerked his head for the musician to come further into the room.

As people saw the fiddler, the buzz of conversation stilled. Earlier, Michael had spread the word about what he wanted for the first dance, and now people obliged by moving out of the parlor and leaving floor space.

Prudence stood with her back to the entry, talking to the Garrs. At that moment, Cecelia looked past her and smiled.

His wife swung around. "What's going on?"

"Another surprise." Michael extended a hand to her. "This one's for us, my dear."

"Whatever do you mean?" Even as Prudence asked the question, she slipped her gloved hand into his.

Michael pulled her into a closed dance position, liking her proximity, and slipped an arm around her waist. He hadn't waltzed in years, but when he'd still lived at home with his family, he'd been a sought-after partner at parties.

In a waltz, a couple can flow together, or a poor dancer can make the experience a misery. He'd had both types of partners. *I wonder which Prudence will be.*

Before his bride had time to protest, Michael nodded at Obadiah, who obediently struck up the strains of the waltz.

She gasped. "Waldteufel in Morgan's Crossing? I heard the St. Louis Philharmonic play this last year."

"Obadiah used to play in an orchestra." *Until they kicked him out for drunkenness.* "He has quite a repertoire." Without elaborating further, Michael swung her into the waltz.

Obediently, she accompanied him. "Aren't the others going to dance?"

"Not this one. They'll squeeze in later."

Michael assumed his wife was accustomed to dancing in ballrooms with plenty of space, but she followed his tight turns around the parlor without a hitch. He'd forgotten the intimacy of the waltz—the sensual feel of her waist under his hand, the dizzying smell of her perfume, moving together as one.

With sparkling blue-green eyes, pink cheeks, and a wide smile, Prudence radiated happiness, just as a bride should.

Michael found himself drawn to her, reveling in the fact that *he* was the man bringing her joy.

With a flourish, Obadiah drew the waltz to a close and swung his bow into the air.

Michael slowed their steps but didn't release Prudence, staring into her eyes until a thunderous wave of applause made them pull apart. He kept ahold of her hand. "Now for a polka," he called, beckoning with his free hand. "Come join us, everyone." He gestured to Obadiah to start the music and drew Prudence closer.

She grasped a fold of her skirt, and he swept her into the dance. They only had a single turn about the room at the polka's bouncing speed before husbands caught up their wives, two men grabbed Marla and Becky Lee, and Dean pulled his mother onto the floor. Even Juanita and Bobby galloped around the room. With so little space and inexperienced dancers, often Michael had to abruptly stop and start, turning sharply to avoid colliding with moving people.

Prudence surprised him by letting out peals of laughter, clutching him when they appeared about to crash. Tendrils of hair escaped her pins to wisp around her glowing face.

When the dance ended, she placed a hand to her chest. "No more, Michael, I beg you," she gasped. "I must catch my breath."

He laughed. Keeping an arm around her waist, he guided his wife out of the parlor and into the hall.

The watchers moved out of the way. Others swirled around them as the miners rushed to find partners. The women would be danced off their feet, changing partners with each song so every man would have at least one chance. Portia Rossmore was the sole exception, standing next to her husband, casting furtive glances at the whirling couples. The rest of the men knew better than to solicit her for a turn around the floor.

As she and Michael watched the dancers bounding around

the room, Prudence waved her hand in front of her face to cool herself. "I should have brought my fan. You didn't warn me we'd have dancing."

"I wanted to surprise you."

"You did!" Prudence placed a hand on his arm and squeezed. "I've never enjoyed a dance so much."

"Nor I, my dear." To his amazement, Michael realized he'd just told the truth—not some social lie for the sake of politeness, or to further his plan to get her into his bed.

Her lips parted.

Michael couldn't resist leaning to drop a kiss on her mouth. "To many more, later." He made his tone full of promise.

"To many more," she whispered, her gaze soft.

For a moment, he wished they were alone to pursue kisses and explore each other's bodies. But there'd be time later to finish out the party in an intimate fashion.

The music ended, and Michael led Prudence over to Obadiah, stopping far enough away so she hopefully wouldn't smell the whiskey on his breath or his stale body odor. "Obadiah Kettering, our fiddler."

"Mr. Kettering, I didn't expect to hear such a fine violin performance in Morgan's Crossing."

"Ah, thank you, ma'am," he slurred, his green eyes blurry. He rocked forward.

A bad feeling cramped Michael's gut. He reached to pull his wife farther away from the fiddler. But he wasn't fast enough.

With a gurgling sound, Obadiah placed a hand to his stomach, leaning forward to upchuck all over her gown.

Prudence screamed, and Michael cursed, knowing the drunken sot had just ruined his plans for the rest of the evening.

Chapter Fifteen

The morning after the party, Prudence couldn't bring herself to get out of bed. Normally, she arose as soon as she awoke, but today she couldn't bear to face the reality of living in Morgan's Crossing. She shuddered at the memory of last night's dreadful ending—the ruination of her beautiful dress; her screams of disgust and outrage; her husband cursing the fiddler, using language that shocked her; Mrs. Tisdale and Mrs. Rivera hustling her upstairs to help her get clean and taking the fouled gown with them; her refusal to speak to Michael when he came to her bedroom door.

For several hours, I was so happy.

Doubts and delights, one after another, with the doubts winning, she repeated her thoughts from the night before. Her heart ached with what might have been. *Doubts had, indeed, vanquished the delight of the party.*

Prudence turned her face from the windows, not wanting to see the rosy glow of the early morning. Her stomach rumbled, but she had no energy to move from the bed to dress and feed herself. Instead, her thoughts trod familiar paths as she tried to figure out what to do with her life. But she came full circle to where she was right now. *I have no family and friends to turn to, little money and no skills to support myself.*

I have nowhere to go. The realization had never brought such a bleak feeling of powerlessness, and Prudence wondered just how long she could remain right here and avoid facing her life. *I could go into a decline.* The fantasy of wasting away in bed, the object of concern, appealed to her. But she knew she'd become bored after only a few hours.

As much as I don't want to live in Morgan's Crossing, at least for now I'm stuck here. Therefore, I must make this place more to my liking. She began mulling over her list of needed changes—her home, the store, and a school. Organizing her ideas gave Prudence some much-needed energy.

Michael said I'd initiate welcome changes to this town, so I'd best get started. The first thing I need to do is go shopping. I'll wrest the catalogue from Mr. Hugely and place an order.

The idea galvanized her. Pushing back the bed coverings, Prudence put her feet on the polished planks and stood. In keeping with her plans to implement change, she resolved to make a show of her forthcoming appearance in town—give people something else to think about besides last night's disaster. She eyed the purple outfit, shirtwaist and skirt hanging from clothespins on the rope stretched across the end of her bed—her makeshift wardrobe. *I'll start with that.*

Prudence washed up, dressed, and combed her hair as quickly as possible. She completed her ensemble with the matching hat, which she secured with a hatpin. Then she pinned a gold watch to her chest. She checked her appearance in her hand mirror, making a mental note to order a large looking glass first thing.

As a final touch, she strode to the closest trunk and took out the purple parasol she'd ordered to match her dress. Prudence unfurled it, running her fingers over the ruffled lace edging. Just for fun, she held the parasol over her head, spun the handle, and minced out of the room.

Once on the landing, she looked downstairs and listened for Michael. No chairs remained in the entry and hallway. Everyone must have taken theirs' home after the party, or her husband had organized the miners to return them.

The house was silent, and she figured Michael had already left for the mine. With a small stab of guilt, she wondered if he'd eaten at the boarding house again. *I'd rather starve than eat at that place.*

Through the glass in the doors, she saw movement on the porch and moved to the parlor window to check.

Juanita Rivera took a seat on the porch step.

Why would a child come visiting? And so early, too?

Prudence propped her parasol in a corner and hurried outside. "Juanita, whatever are you doing here?" With a pang, she noted the red lanterns were gone, and the memory of her first kiss quivered in her stomach. She forced her attention to Juanita, who wore a faded gray pinafore over a washed-out pink dress.

The child stood, her wide-eyed dark gaze taking in Prudence's purple outfit. "*Ave Maria,*" she said on an awed breath. Her hand fluttered toward the skirt, but she didn't touch the material. "So pretty. You look like a *queen,* Mrs. Morgan."

"You dear child," Prudence said, touched by the girl's sincerity.

"I could look at you *all* day."

She chuckled, yet unexpected tears pricked her eyes. On impulse, she stooped to give Juanita a hug. Straightening, feeling sudden melancholy, Prudence realized she couldn't remember ever hugging anyone. *Surely Lissa and I hugged?* But if they had, those memories were lost in time.

Prudence wrenched her attention to the present. "Now—" she made her tone sound bright "—tell me what has you appearing on my doorstep so early in the morning?"

Juanita held up a battered slate and a tattered book. "I heard Mamá telling Papi that you are an educated lady."

"I am." Seeing the child's earnestness, Prudence suppressed her smile.

"I want help with some words."

That's odd. "Why doesn't your mother help you?"

"She doesn't know how to read. Neither does Papi."

130

"But who has taught you this much?"

"Mrs. Copelin and Mrs. Garr take turns teaching us. But they are busy and say they don't know much more than what we've learned already."

This town needs a teacher. Prudence tallied up the number of school-age children she'd seen the night before—Juanita, Bobby, Rufus, the three Copelin boys whose names she hadn't learned. She wondered at the age of the Oriental boys who worked at the boarding house. *A small school, indeed, but still necessary.*

She held open the door for the child. "Come inside, Juanita, and I'll see what I can do." Once in the house, Prudence led the child into the study and took a seat at the desk, pulling up another chair next to her. She patted the seat.

Juanita scooted into the chair and set her book, slate, and a stubby piece of chalk on the desk.

"Now, child. Show me what's the problem." Prudence picked up the book and glanced at the title. "Ah, *Little Women.* One of my favorites when I was your age. In fact, I brought it with me along with several more books by this author." She opened to the first page and began to read aloud. "'Christmas won't be Christmas without any presents,' grumbled Jo, lying on the rug.'"

Dark eyes bright with enthusiasm, Juanita clapped her hands together and bounced on her seat. "More, please."

Prudence caught the child's infectious spirit. "How about this?" She tapped the page where she'd left off. "We'll read together. I'll read a paragraph, and then you'll read a paragraph. I'll help you sound out any word you don't know. When I was about your age, I did that with my older sister using this very story." For the first time, the memory of Lissa didn't sting.

"Oh, *yes,* ma'am." Juanita bent over the book and followed Prudence's finger, continuing the story.

They read back and forth, sometimes stopping to write a word on the slate so Juanita could copy it later.

Prudence was engrossed with her teaching, when she heard the sound of the bell at the door. Realizing that at least half an

131

hour at least must have passed, she shifted to see through the window.

Mrs. Tisdale waved, and then held up a basket.

Prudence motioned for the woman to enter.

Mrs. Tisdale huffed through the door and hurried over to set the basket on the desk. "Good morning, Mrs. Morgan. You're up with the birds. And here I thought you'd need your sleep this fine day."

"Thank you for your concern, Mrs. Tisdale. I have too much to do to lay abed." She shifted and gestured to Juanita. "First of all this child is telling me she needs help with her schooling. Why didn't she go to you?"

"Goodness me, Mrs. Morgan." She nodded at Juanita. "I know enough to write my name, spell out words, and do my accounts, but not enough to teach the children. Mrs. Garr and Mrs. Copelin both attended school for a few years, so they do what they can."

A few years. Prudence had taken having a governess for granted—for being able to read what she wanted, to calculate numbers, know history, to speak a foreign language—*not that French would be the least bit of use here.*

Mrs. Tisdale unpacked the basket, laying out the silverware, a plate with bacon, scrambled eggs, and toast, and a jam jar with coffee. "The children's lessons are hit or miss, though, seeing as both ladies have their hands full attending to their own families."

"I see." *That will not do.* "Well, I'll certainly have to bring this up with Mr. Morgan. This town needs a school."

Mrs. Tisdale gave her an approving smile. "I do believe, Mrs. Morgan, you just may be the best thing to happen here in a long while."

Prudence sat straighter. "I certainly hope so. Thank you for bringing my breakfast."

"No problem at all. And I left a rabbit pie in the springhouse for you to heat up for dinner. Now, I'm a thinkin' you'll want to start doing some cookin' yourself."

Not particularly. "I believe I'll wait until the kitchen is well stocked. I intend to place a large order today."

"Of course." Mrs. Tisdale pointed to the basket. "Like I said yesterday, don't bother washing the dishes." She gestured to Juanita. "Come along, child. Let's leave Mrs. Morgan to eat in peace."

The girl jumped to her feet and gathered her slate and book. "Thank you, ma'am," she said with obvious adoration.

Ma'am. Another new title.

Feeling genuine affection for the girl, Prudence smiled. "You're welcome, Juanita. Come tomorrow, and we'll continue."

With bouncing, tiptoeing steps, the young girl sashayed to the door, obviously dancing her delight.

With a smile, Prudence watched Juanita, surprised by feeling an emotion of—what she imagined—was maternal warmth. She'd never liked children, always looking at them as bothersome creatures. *Like my parents did me.* She was struck by the sudden realization and wondered what other aspects of her nature were due to her family.

Mrs. Tisdale bade her good day and bustled away.

Prudence began to eat, pondering her list. When she finished breakfast, she packed everything into the basket, grabbed her parasol, and strolled out the front door. Once outside, she hesitated, not wanting to carry both the basket and the parasol. She had a vision in mind for this particular stroll, and the basket didn't fit. And, really, she required two hands to properly hold the handle and best display her complete outfit.

On his way to the boarding house for breakfast—with too many problems jumping around in his brain like fleas on a mangy dog—Michael realized he needed to be alone, away from his wife, his miners, and the rest of the townsfolk. In the past when he'd felt this way, he could just go home. But now

Prudence's presence meant his house was no longer a refuge, and he needed to travel farther afield.

To the river, he thought with a sudden burst of inspiration and went digging for his fishing gear, stored in the stable. *I'll catch enough trout for dinner for both the Tisdales and us.*

The manly excuse of providing food for his family—*how strange to think of calling me and Prudence a family*—picked up his spirits and went a ways to easing any guilt at the thought of playing hooky from work. That was until Michael walked into the stable and ran into tall, lankie Howie, who like usual had blended into the shadows near the first stall.

The stableman nodded. "Mornin', boss. Got King all saddled up and ready to go."

Michael debated with himself. As much as he wanted to sneak off, he had responsibilities and should let someone at the mine know his plans. "I'm going fishing instead of to the mine. If you need to find me, I'll be by the triangle rock. After last night's party, I need to restock the larder."

Howie raised an eyebrow but said nothing.

Both of them knew fishing was a dicey business. Michael was just as likely to come home empty-handed as he was to catch a mess of trout. But as excuses went, it wasn't half bad.

Michael jerked his head in the direction of the mine. "You ride on up and tell Rossmore…No. Tell Cal Johnson—" he chose his other foreman as the better man to leave in charge. "I won't be in today. Tell him to take all precautions for the men's sake."

"Will do, boss." The stableman moved into the second stall, and then popped out again. "Seeing as you don't have a food parcel and all, you want some venison jerky to take along?"

"That would be good." Michael gave the stableman a genuine smile. Howie was a man of few words, but he had a loyal streak, often noticing and taking care of Michael's needs without being asked. *A rare quality—almost wife-like—and one my bride doesn't seem to possess.* The discouraging thought blighted his enthusiasm.

Howie nodded and backed into the stall to saddle the other gelding.

Lost in thought about loyalty, solicitousness, and what those qualities might mean to a marriage, Michael absently gathered the flat-sided creel, rake for digging worms, extra hooks, and his pole, with hook and line already strung. He greeted King by rubbing the horse's head and secured everything but the pole to the saddle. He led the gelding outside and mounted up, pole in hand.

Michael turned the gelding in the direction of the mine, preferring to take the long way to his favorite fishing spot, rather than ride through town, where he might have to stop and explain himself to anyone catching sight of him. He wanted solitude to mull over his marriage and find a way to manage his wife. He refused to live on tenterhooks, unhappy and always worried.

He reconsidered. *On the other hand, I need time alone to not think about my marriage.* After a few hours on the river, he then could turn his attention back to the problem of Prudence and try to figure out what to do next. *There must be a way to coax the laughing woman I danced with last night to come out from behind the wall she's put between us.*

Chapter Sixteen

In a modified version of Juanita's sashay, Prudence swanned up the street. The day was perfect for a stroll, sunny and warm with some feathered clouds stretching across the rich blue sky. She'd been told, that in Montana Territory, sunshine from now on was a blessing, but she couldn't imagine a snowstorm descending in September.

Too bad Morgan's Crossing doesn't have a park with trees and grass and flowers. Still watching the clouds, Prudence added the idea to her list—at the bottom, of course—but, nevertheless, a pleasant dream. She made a note to plant a seed in her husband's mind when she discussed her other topics with him.

"Mrs. Morgan!"

Startled by the shrillness of the call, Prudence jerked and whirled, her heartbeat speeding up.

Mrs. Tisdale, one hand clapped to her straw hat, the other holding up her skirts in an unsightly manner, hurried toward her, her expression fearful. A heavy, crocheted reticule hung from her arm.

Corresponding alarm tightened Prudence's stomach. *There's been an accident at the mine!* Fear stabbed her. *Please, not Michael!* Guilt followed. *I shouldn't have refused to talk to him after the party.* She quickened her steps to meet the woman. "What's wrong?"

Mrs. Tisdale stumbled to a stop, her generous bosom heaving. "It's Portia Rossmore's time!" she gasped out.

Prudence exhaled in relief. *Not Michael then.*

"I heard her screaming and went to their door, but that brute of a husband won't let me in! Every man who can intervene is deep in the mine. By the time I send Bobby to the mine, he tracks down his father or the boss and they make their way, and then hightail back to town, their arrival might be too late for Portia or the baby. I don't know how long she's been laboring."

"Oh, dear Lord!" She wasn't sure if the words were a prayer or a curse. "What about a doctor?" Even as she asked, Prudence realized the ridiculous nature of her question. If this town had a physician, she would have met him by now. *How can I possibly live in a town with no doctor?*

"One of the newer miners, Rye Rawlins, he is, doctors us up when need be—cuts and broken limbs and such." Mrs. Tisdale drew a deep breath. "But I'm the one who's delivered every babe in this place."

Determination welled up in Prudence. "And you shall this one, too." She snapped her parasol shut. "Come with me." In the quickest march she could manage with her corset tied so tightly, she stormed down the street.

Mrs. Tisdale huffed to keep up. "The Rossmores live two houses down from mine," she said, gesturing.

Prudence hurried to the one Mrs. Tisdale indicated. Blistered brown paint covered the door, peeling off in places. No flowers grew around the entrance. With a fist, she pounded on the door, dislodging a few chips. She waited a few seconds, and then pounded again.

"Clyde's closed the windows," Mrs. Tisdale said between breaths. "Probably so no one else will hear and try to interfere."

The door flew open. Clyde Rossmore, his hair sticking up in clumps, thrust his head out. "Go away," he growled. His breath stank of alcohol.

Inwardly, Prudence quailed at the antipathy in his eyes and took a step back. But a strangled cry from inside the home turned her spine to iron. "We will not!" she snapped. "Let us in this *instant*, so Mrs. Tisdale can attend to your wife."

Clyde shifted his footing to close the door.

Realizing his intent, Prudence acted without thinking, jamming the point of her parasol into his stomach as hard as she could.

Startled, the bully stumbled back, his hands covering his middle.

He's obviously not used to opposition, for my blow couldn't have hurt that much.

Prudence took advantage of the opportunity to shove past him. Once inside, she moved into the center of the room to stand near a small table covered with a faded red-checked cloth, her parasol held in front of her like a sword.

With a growl, Clyde followed her, which allowed Mrs. Tisdale to enter and move behind him, bee-lining to the bed in the corner where Portia lay. With his malevolent attention focused on Prudence, he didn't seem to notice the presence of the older woman.

Even though her knees shook with fear, Prudence drew herself up, summoning her most imperious air. "Birthing a baby is *women's* business, Clyde Rossmore." With a flick of her wrist, she gestured toward the door. "You take yourself off. Go about *men's* business, for goodness sake. Aren't you supposed to be at the mine now? We'll summon you when the child has arrived."

He clenched his fists. "Get out before I throw you out."

"Don't you raise a hand to me," Prudence warned, her tone sharp enough to cut. With rock-solid certainty, she declared, "Mr. Morgan may not be able to prevent you from beating *your* wife, but he can and certainly will punish you for touching *his* wife!"

The wild glare in his pale gray eyes made Prudence tighten her grip on her parasol, but she kept her regal façade in place, determined not to show him any sign of fear. She'd once seen that look on a rabid dog before the creature charged a man, savagely biting him. She'd been walking with Papa, and he'd thrust her behind him. Until now, she'd forgotten that moment—the thrill of feeling protected by the father who'd usually been so distant. *Now I'm the one who has to protect us.*

Hands curled as if to wrap around her throat, Clyde rushed her.

With a two-handed grip, Prudence raised her parasol and, with all her might, brought it down on his head, feeling the impact reverberate up her arms.

The parasol snapped. The end dangled, held together only by the purple material.

Clyde staggered back, putting a hand to his bleeding forehead and staring with dazed eyes. For a moment, at least, the fight seemed to have oozed out of him.

"Leave!" Prudence commanded in a thunderous tone, knowing she needed to get Clyde out of the house before he managed to regroup. With a dramatic flourish, she pointed to the open door with the broken parasol. "Do not return until this child is born!"

With a murderous glare, the brute stomped from the cabin, slamming the door behind him. The structure shook, but then calm settled on the room, broken only by Portia's gasping, pain-filled breaths.

Prudence bounded to the door and dropped the wooden bar in place, locking the man out of his own home. She leaned her back against the wall, knees weak, feeling sick.

"Good riddance to that rubbish." Mrs. Tisdale dusted her hands. "Very well handled, my dear Mrs. Morgan." She lifted her chin to indicate the rifle on pegs over the door. "He'll need an axe to get back in. And if he tries, we'll use that on him."

The older woman's bracing tone instilled strength in Prudence. She took the deepest breath her corset would allow and staggered away from the wall, trying to hide how shaken she was.

Mrs. Tisdale moved to drop her reticule on the table, and then went back to the bed. "Let me take a look at you, dear." She flipped the bed coverings from Portia's body and drew up the nightgown over her bent knees.

Uncomfortable with the woman's nakedness, Prudence looked away, examining the cabin. With only one bed, the room had more space than the Tisdales, which wasn't much. The furnishings seemed plain, and she could discern no objects that held pride of place—no photographs or pictures, no knickknacks, not even a Mason jar with flowers. *Such a pitifully stark existence.*

"Please heat some water, Mrs. Morgan," Mrs. Tisdale directed. "This child will be here any time now, and we must be prepared."

Prudence moved to a small round stove that was badly in need of blacking. Grateful for her experience at the agency, she worked quickly to add wood and light the kindling. Luckily, the kettle was already full, so she didn't have to leave to search for water, for she saw no pump. *Where do they get their water? A well? The river?*

Portia's cry of pain pierced through Prudence. Stilling, she glanced toward the bed.

The woman raised her shoulders. Her head bent forward, mouth open, making unearthly groans and gasping noises.

Mrs. Tisdale moved to the bottom of the bed and leaned over Portia's bent knees to check the status of the baby. "That's it, Portia, dear. You're doing just fine." After the contraction eased, the older woman moved to the stove and poured warm water into a basin. She soaped her hands, drying them on a clean towel with tattered edges that she took from a stack on the narrow kitchen counter. With a jerk of her head, she motioned for Prudence to do the same.

With a wince at what the harsh lye soap would do to her skin, she followed suit, and then emptied the water from the basin into a slops pail.

"I have some dried herbs in my reticule, Mrs. Morgan. Please get them out and steep them for later. They'll help stop the bleeding."

In the reticule on the table, Prudence found a brown-paper packet of herbs tied close with twine. "All of these?"

"Yes, those." Mrs. Tisdale returned to Portia's side.

Prudence found a battered tin cup in the cupboard, dropped in the herbs, and poured hot water over them.

Mrs. Tisdale shot Prudence a quick glance and motioned her over to the bed. "Take her hand. A woman needs something to hold onto at a time like this."

Her heart pounding, Prudence obeyed.

Portia's hand was delicate, her skin rough, palm calloused. She clung to Prudence as if to a lifeline.

The next hour passed in a blur of tension as Prudence watched the age-old struggle of a woman fighting to give birth. A dozen times, she vowed to herself *never* to bear a child. Her hand throbbed from the pressure of Portia's iron grip, her skin bloody with crescent marks. But she didn't move from the woman's side, engrossed with every fiber of her being in helping this baby be born, even if she could only provide emotional strength. She leaned over Portia to dab a cloth over her perspiring face.

The woman gave a harsh cry and curled her body forward.

"Brace her shoulders," Mrs. Tisdale ordered. "The babe's coming."

Heedless of her new dress, Prudence sat behind Portia on the bed, propping the woman against her body.

Portia made animal-sounding grunts as she pushed out the baby.

"That's it. Almost here." Mrs. Tisdale held her hands between Portia's legs as the baby slithered out. "A girl. A beautiful, beautiful girl." Gently, she cradled the child to her bosom.

An ungainly gray cord dangled from the baby's stomach to between Portia's legs.

With the infant held in the crook of her arm, Mrs. Tisdale grabbed up a cloth and gave the baby's head and face a quick, gentle wipe.

The infant wiggled and let out a cry.

"There, there." Mrs. Tisdale leaned forward to place the babe in her mother's outstretched arms.

"My baby." Crying, Portia brought her daughter to her chest.

As she watched the new mother sob with apparent relief and joy, tears welled in Prudence's eyes and rolled down her cheeks.

Portia kissed the baby's forehead and examined her daughter, unfurling miniature fingers and toes. "She's perfect."

"That she is," Mrs. Tisdale agreed with a smile. "You did just marvelous, my dear." She busied herself with cutting and tying off the cord. She disposed of the cord and afterbirth in the slops pail, before washing her hands and picking up the tin cup of herbal tea.

Prudence pulled a handkerchief from her sleeve, thankful she had the forethought to bring one along. *All those years of Mama reminding me to be sure to always carry a clean handkerchief....* After this experience she would forever view motherhood differently. *Such a vast responsibility.* She wiped the tears from her face and blew her nose, realizing that perhaps she wasn't as loath to be a mother someday, after all.

With a maternal glow, Portia smiled down at the babe, but her eyes remained shadowed. "Clyde will beat me for delivering a girl. He was so sure we'd have a son." She kissed her baby's head. "But I don't care. I'm so thankful for my sweet daughter."

This time the tears pricking Prudence's eyes were different than before. She felt a profound helplessness at Portia's situation—indeed, for all women tied to men who were legally allowed to abuse them—as well experienced as a deep sadness that a father would not welcome the gift of a beautiful daughter.

Mrs. Tisdale pulled the table next to the bed and set the cup of tea by Portia's shoulder. She leaned over to touch the baby's cheek. "What will you name her?"

Portia glanced at the older woman and then at Prudence. Her smile held sadness. "I want my daughter to grow up strong. Not scared and weak like me. I'll call her *Prudence.*" Her gaze swung to Mrs. Tisdale. "May. Prudence May."

Mrs. Tisdale placed a hand to her ample chest. "I'm honored."

Although she was touched by Portia's choice as well as the new mother's belief in her strength, Prudence shook her head.

"Oh, no, you won't. You will *not* saddle your sweet baby with a horrid name like mine, even if Clyde would allow you to after I broke my parasol over his head. But—" she choked on an unexpected sob, covered her mouth, and had to catch her breath. "I had a sister who was dear to me. Lissa. I'd be honored if you'd use her name."

"Lissa," Portia whispered with a smile. "She shall be Lissa May."

An hour after Lissa May's birth, Prudence sat at the desk in Michael's study. Mrs. Tisdale had shooed her off from the Rossmores' home, saying Portia needed to rest, and she'd remain to take care of her. The plate containing the remains of a slice of rabbit pie was pushed to one corner while she perused the Montgomery Ward catalogue she'd wrested from Mr. Hugely's clutches.

Waiting until the man went into his private room to retrieve the catalogue, Prudence had swiped the store ledger, hiding it behind her back before the man returned and managing to spirit the records from the store. She also memorized the prices on some of the goods.

I've won a lot of battles today!

Pleased with herself, Prudence paged through the catalogue and chose the best quality merchandise that suited her taste. Then she jotted down the price on a piece of stationery—for she didn't have any other paper—as well as the page number where the item was to be found.

She'd torn another sheet of stationery into long strips, labeling each one and tucking it between the pages of the catalogue to mark her choices. She wanted to make sure everything she selected was also to Michael's taste. A couple of pieces she was prepared to compromise on, but she intended to put her foot down on the rest.

Prudence struggled the most with what she needed for the

kitchen, wishing she'd thought to itemize everything Mrs. Seymour's contained. Mentally, she went through the agency's kitchen, cupboard by cupboard, which was stocked full of various pots and pans of different sizes, although Dona and the mail-order brides had only seemed to use the big ones.

Prudence would be mostly cooking for just her and Michael. *Should I order both small and large sizes, or should I just go with the small ones? But if we entertain, I'll need the bigger pots.* She tapped the end of the pen on her chin. *Decisions. Decisions. And not nearly as much fun as shopping for clothes.*

She sighed at the enormity of the task and did the best she could. *I wonder if I sent the list to Dona and asked for her help if she'd add what else I need.* But the cook might as easily toss the paper into the trash. In retrospect, Prudence regretted not being nicer to the woman. *Perhaps if I include a letter of apology....*

By the time she'd finished, the total had grown to an astonishing amount, which made her uneasy. She was about to spend a great deal of her husband's money.

Michael owns a gold mine and several businesses, Prudence assured her conscience. *I'm furnishing our house from top to bottom, including stocking the kitchen with pots, pans, and other utensils I need for cooking and storing food, as well as the supplies themselves....*

Underneath the total for the house, Prudence drew a line across the page and began to list supplies needed for the store, starting with bolts of fabric, including cotton for undergarments and flannel for diapers.

We should buy a gift for Lissa May. She added *baby clothes* to the upper list, and then returned to jotting down more goods for the store. *The women are in need of hats.* She chose some plain straw and felt ones, all of which could be embellished with the ribbons, lace, and netting she added to the list.

What else? Again Prudence tapped the end of the pen on her chin, thinking of objects that would appeal to women, yet that wouldn't sit in the store unsold for months or years. After all, Michael did need to turn a profit from the business. *Yarn, thread, buttons, sewing needles.*

I'll have to ask Mrs. Tisdale if there are some other things to add. Prudence moved on to foodstuffs, starting with cans of peaches, for peach cobbler was a favorite of hers. Probably others also longed for fruit they couldn't grow or pick locally. *Tea. Chocolate.* She smiled. *Both are necessities. Probably should include penny candy as well.*

She thought of the Tisdale and Rossmore homes. Neither had a mirror hanging on the wall. *Hanging mirrors,* she added, although she doubted Clyde would allow Portia such a purchase.

On a second piece of paper, Prudence drew columns for goods she'd seen in the store, such as work gloves, replacement handles for tools, men's clothing, and the like, looking them up in the catalogue and writing down the price, circling those where she knew the prices, drawing lines to others. Later, she planned to compare the prices with the rest of the store's merchandise. *Find out shipping charges,* she scrawled across the bottom of the page.

Two hours later, her task nearly finished, Prudence heard the sound of the front doors, and looked up to see her husband crossing the vestibule. Surprised, she glanced at the watch pinned to her dress. *He's early.* She studied her work. *Good. I can show him everything while the light is still bright.*

Michael walked through the second set of doors carrying a woven basket. His sleeves were rolled up and damp splotches marred his shirt and pants. His skin looked reddened from the sun.

She rose and smiled a welcome.

His eyes widened. Apparently he hadn't expected a greeting. He grinned and folded back the lid of the basket. "Look what I brought you."

Curious, Prudence moved to look inside. The container was full of neatly stacked, beheaded fish. Wrinkling her nose at the smell, she stepped back.

"I cleaned the trout already. They're ready for the frying pan.

"They are very, ah…very *nice* fish."

"*Nice,* eh." His tone held a teasing note.

"Although I'd prefer flowers, fancy chocolate, jewelry…"

"Duly noted, wife. But for now, you'll have to be content with trout for supper."

Prudence was grateful he hadn't brought her the fish alive. The worst lesson she'd endured at the agency was wringing the neck of a chicken, drenching the fowl in boiling water, and then plucking the feathers and cleaning out the insides. The whole time, she'd tried not to breathe in the smell—worse than a wet dog. She shuddered at the memory.

Michael must have noticed the movement, for he tilted his head toward the door. "I'll just put this on the porch. Once he's seen to my horse, Howie's taking the fish to the Tisdale's. But I wanted to show you my catch first."

"Uh, thank you." Gingerly, she extended a hand. "I'll take them outside for you, so you can wash up." She waved toward the desk. "I'm been working on some things, and I'd like to discuss them with you."

His eyebrows pulled together in a frown, but Michael nodded, handing her the basket, and turned to walk down the hall into the kitchen.

The basket's weight was heavier than she'd expected. *But how often have I carried heavy things?* Not even at the agency, when she had the lesson on scrubbing the floor, for Evie had filled the pail of water and brought it to her. A brief stab of regret ran through her for not appreciating how hard the maid had worked. *I shouldn't have been so mean to her.*

As she took the basket of trout outside, Prudence ran down the items she wanted to discuss with her husband. *Too bad I didn't complete my examination of the store's ledger.* From what she'd seen so far, she was certain Hugely was running a scam on her husband. But that would have to be a conversation for another time when she could show Michael the proof.

Thinking of her interaction with Juanita, and the hope she felt for the future of little Lissa May, Prudence chose *education* for the first item of business—once she'd caught him up on the news of the day, of course. A prosaic start, perhaps, but a topic that had today become more meaningful than the new furniture and other decor she'd picked out for their home.

Cecilia Garr was passing the house, and when she saw Prudence on the porch, the woman stopped to chat about Portia's baby.

Amused by the speed gossip had raced around the town and flattered by the woman's obvious admiration, Prudence lingered in conversation. The embellishments given to the story in Mrs. Garr's thick southern accent—Clyde dancing around the house to evade Prudence with her parasol, and then running out the door and down half the street with her chasing him—sounded so funny Prudence laughed until she was in stitches.

I can't remember the last time I laughed until I cried. Wiping moisture from her eyes, she bade the woman good day. Prudence returned to the house, mischievously planning to borrow Mrs. Garr's accent when she regaled Michael with her news.

Chapter Seventeen

Michael was surprised at the relief he felt from Prudence's friendly greeting, even if she wasn't impressed by the trout he'd caught. After the debacle at the end of last night's party, she'd shut herself in the bedroom. He'd assumed he'd face the same cold wife today.

While he washed up at the kitchen sink, Michael wondered if he should mention last night, or pretend nothing happened. After all, he'd already apologized several times to no avail. Prudence, defiled by Obadiah's vomit, had continue to scream until she'd raced upstairs in the dark, followed by Mrs. Tisdale and Mrs. Rivera carrying lamps.

Afterwards, she'd apparently frozen into an icicle of anger and embarrassment, for she'd refused to open the bedroom door or speak to him. He'd had no choice but to bid their guests goodnight and toss restlessly on his pallet in the solitary room, worrying for the future, his marriage—and his sanity.

He clenched his fists, remembering his rage at Obadiah. Only the fact that the fiddler had passed out on the floor kept Michael from punching the man. Even so, he'd ordered Obadiah thrown into the river and told Rigsby the man wasn't to be served liquor until further notice. Once the drunk used up his own stash, he'd be forced to dry out.

Michael glanced at a plate, covered with cheesecloth, issuing scents of Mrs. Tisdale's rabbit pie. His stomach growled, but he figured he should talk to his wife while she was apparently willing to speak with him.

Still unresolved about how to act with Prudence, Michael returned to the study. Through the window, he could see his wife on the porch, leaning over the railing and talking to Cecelia Garr, who had a gleeful expression on her face.

To his surprise, Prudence threw back her head and laughed. Her shoulders shook.

His wife's good spirits made his own rise, and Michael wished he could see her face.

Noticing a catalogue and papers spread out on the desk, he wandered over to see what his wife had been up to. Grasping the paper, he chuckled at the *Mrs. Michael Morgan* calligraphied across the top. *Prudence certainly came prepared for polite society.* His smile faded as he remembered last night. *And unprepared for real life in Morgan's Crossing.*

Standing mirror, written at the top of the list, caught his eye, followed by the price. *What in tarnation?*

Michael scanned the rest of the items, and the total, coming in at close to a thousand dollars, made a slow burn in his chest. He couldn't believe some of the frivolities his wife intended to purchase. *Fabric? Lace? Ribbons?* Prudence had brought *four* trunks with her. Judging from the clothing he'd seen so far, she certainly possessed enough. Plenty of nice dresses hung on the rope Howie had tied across her bed. To his mind, his wife had no need for more for the foreseeable future.

Chocolate. Prudence wasn't kidding when she'd said she preferred fancy chocolates as gifts. He scanned the list for jewelry but thankfully didn't see any. *Yet.* The list didn't look complete.

Hanging mirrors caught his eye. *Standing mirrors, hanging mirrors! At this rate, she'll have one in every room of the house. How vain could the woman be?*

He read on. *Canned peaches? What is wrong with good ole Montana Territory fruit?*

Hats—two straw and three felts. He glanced at a fancy straw bonnet covered with netting and lace hanging on a coat hook by the front door, the purple a splash of color against the white paint.

Michael couldn't believe how selfish and wasteful her list was. *She'll squander all my money.* He'd expected they'd have a discussion about what was needed for the house, prioritizing things such as a kitchen table and chairs and buy items little-by-little, not in one huge extravagant fell swoop.

His stomach sinking, Michael realized, *I made the biggest mistake of my life when I married Prudence Crawford.*

With quick strides, he crossed the room to a shelf holding his whiskey and poured himself a glass, emptying the bottle. *I neglected to stock my liquor cabinet at the same time I wrote for a mail-order bride. Foolish of me.* He took a big gulp instead of his usual sip. The whiskey burned down his throat. Instead of calming the heat in his stomach, the liquor only served to fan the flames of his anger.

Prudence rushed into the house, a broad smile on her face. The purple dress she wore turned her eyes lavender, and obvious excitement flushed her cheeks.

Probably ecstatic about spending my gold.

"Michael, I've had the most *interesting* day."

"I'm sure you have," he said, sarcastically.

Prudence didn't seem to notice his wry tone for her smile remained in place, her eyes bright. "This morning Juanita Rivera appeared on our doorstep, asking for my help with reading *Little Women.* So we started through the book together. That child is so intelligent, which put me in mind of the need for a school here." She gazed at him, an expectant look on her face.

Another item on her list. He sipped his whiskey. "A schoolteacher is expensive. I don't see the need, for only six children."

The glowing expression faded from her face. She glanced at the glass in his hand, her eyebrows pinching in disapproval. "Six children of *your town* are growing up without an education."

"Hardly without any education. I know some of the women have been teaching them."

"Women with only *two years* of schooling! Morgan's Crossing needs a *real* teacher."

"I plan to hire one when ten children are of school age."

Her brow furrowed. "Michael, that won't be for several years. The older children need an education *now*."

He clenched his jaw. "Won't do much good to have a teacher, anyway, Prudence. Think about it. Where would she live? Certainly not alone. There's no space for a woman in any house but ours. Are you prepared to board a schoolmarm?"

By her frown, he deduced Prudence didn't like the idea of sharing her home with a teacher, for all that she claimed to want one so much.

"We could build a room onto one of the cabins—the Garrs perhaps."

Michael shook his head. "Not only that, a young single woman in a mining camp overflowing with unmarried men. What do you think will happen?"

"The men will court her."

"Exactly. Distract them is what she'll do. Mining's dangerous work, and they need to keep their minds on the job."

"Oh, for heaven's sake. What a poor excuse."

Michael ignored her. "And it won't just be the miners after her. Women are scarce in Sweetwater Springs, too. Why else do you think so many of us are sending away for mail-order brides?" he said in a self-depreciating tone, envying the three men who'd ended up in happy marriages with amiable wives. "You'll have men coming from miles around to court the teacher. Why, I doubt she'll last a month before getting herself hitched, and you know married women don't teach. Then I'll be out the money of getting her here in the first place, much less paying her salary."

"You could hire a male teacher."

"I'd have to pay him more than a woman," he scoffed.

Her eyes narrowed. "So you're saying this all comes down to you being too *cheap* to pay for a schoolteacher?"

The barb hit, sparking his temper. "That is exactly what I'm saying." He annunciated every word. "You're an educated woman. *You* teach the children."

"Don't be ridiculous," she snapped, her shoulders rigid. "You're just saying that to avoid paying for a real teacher. I can't *abide* a stingy man!"

"Well, you'll have to abide this one, *wife*." He crossed to the desk, picked up her list and flapped the paper under her nose. "And, as your *miserly* husband, I command that you cross off most of these items. Pick only the essentials. I'm not made of money you know."

She gaped at him and swept an arm through the air. "We have *nothing* in this house! You have a store that's shameful in how dirty and lacking it is! The people here, especially the women and children, need *more*."

With his gaze on Prudence, Michael picked up his glass and swallowed the last of the whiskey. "Shall we change your prunes-and-prisms name to Reckless? Spendthrift?" he said in a aloof tone. "*Prudence* doesn't really suit you, my dear, for all you pretend to be so caring."

She raised her pointed chin, and her meager chest expanded.

He gazed at her dispassionately, noting how anger flushed her cheeks and lent brilliance to her pale lavender eyes, making her bony face look almost pretty. "You don't like that suggestion?" he asked in a tone of mock concern. "How about Heedless? Selfish?"

"Michael, you own a *gold* mine."

"Which I'm sure is why you married me."

Her eyes flashed. "I married you because I believed your lies. I thought you were a man of *honor!*"

That blow hit. He looked down at his hand drawn into a fist, not letting her see the hurt. He forced his fingers to uncurl. "I pay my miners their wages and have all the other costs associated with running the mine...and the town. I carry that store on my back. The place loses money as many months as it makes a profit. Now you're adding to the burden with your lavish ways." He met her gaze. "Well, I won't have it. I will not allow your purchases."

"Why——" Her mouth thinned as if holding back a retort.

Michael could only feel relief in not having to brace himself to take another cut from her sharp tongue. He shrugged, turned, and strode toward the door, pulling his coat off the hook by the purple hat and putting it on.

Prudence watched his preparations in dismay. "Don't you walk out on me!" Her voice rose, and she fisted her hands on her hips. "Where are you going?"

"Where any man goes to escape a shrewish wife." Michael clapped the hat on his head.

"The saloon?"

"No, the pigpens." He flung open the inner double doors and strode out, snapping them closed hard enough to make the windows rattle.

Speechless, Prudence stared at the closed door, hurt and anger churning within her. The argument had so caught her off guard that she hadn't even had a chance to defend herself, much less explain. She wanted to run after her husband and pound her fists on his chest until he listened to her reasoning. *No, it wouldn't behoove me as first lady to run down the street screeching after my husband.*

Pigpens? Why would he go there? Prudence didn't recall even seeing any, but then again, she hadn't explored the whole town, particularly the area near the tents at the outskirts. *Did he mean pigpens as a metaphorical jab at me?* She remembered and again felt the humiliation of being soiled by Obadiah. The thought hurt and made her want to track down Michael and demand he explain just what he meant.

She eyed the account books, left open on the desk. *No, I have better things to do. I need to find out more about the store. Maybe if I have more proof to show him.*

And if he still doesn't listen?

I could always hit him over the head with the broken parasol.

Cheered by the nonsensical image, Prudence set to work.

There weren't many more items from the store that she could remember, but she wrote them down and looked up the prices in the catalogue.

When Prudence finished, she set the pen into the inkwell. *I can't do anything more without a complete survey of the store and gaining knowledge of shipping costs.*

She massaged her cramped hand, frowning at the ink stains on her fingers. Usually she was so careful to dip the pen into the inkwell with the right precision and lightly touched the quill to the paper to avoid any blots. But in her distress and hurry, she'd jabbed the pen into the ink and slashed items and numbers across the page. No one looking at the blots and hen scratches would know she usually wrote in perfect copperplate.

The research had calmed her, and Prudence felt she could now approach her husband without abusing him with a parasol or biting his nose off. She stood and stretched, moving to the back of the house to use the privy. When she'd finished, she washed her hands under the water pump in the sink, grateful to have one indoors—unlike Portia Rossmore. But even with scrubbing, the ink stains remained. *Oh, well. My gloves will hide them.*

Her mind on what she'd say to Michael, she went upstairs to fetch her gloves. She eyed the broken parasol that earlier she'd tossed next to her trunk and realized she'd forgotten to add a new one to the shopping list. *Surely, when Michael learns why I need a new parasol, he'll relent on his ultimatum to severely edit my shopping list.* She tucked a clean handkerchief into her sleeve.

Perhaps I should have a special umbrella made with a reinforced shaft so if I need to use a weapon again, it won't break. The sarcasm cheered her, and she left the room to go downstairs. She donned her hat, anchoring it with the hatpin, and sallied forth to hunt down her husband.

Outside Rigsby's Saloon, the door wide open, Prudence slowed her steps, thinking it would make more sense for Michael to have gone there rather then the pigpens. But she could hardly venture inside and find out. Heavy male laughter and the clinking of glass sealed her decision. Ladies didn't frequent such places.

A miner she didn't know stopped and politely touched his hat. He was obviously headed into the saloon. "Good afternoon, Mrs. Morgan." The man had deep-set eyes, thick brow ridges, and a heavy chin, giving him the look of a troll. While he'd obviously washed up, for his face and hands were clean, his clothes were covered in dust.

"Good afternoon." She hesitated then plunged into conversation. "Forgive me, sir, for not remembering your name."

He grinned, showing gaps in his teeth. "Percy Phillips, ma'am. My shift at the mine is done, and uh…" He gestured toward the bar sounds.

The cultured name was at odds with his appearance, but Prudence was too focused on her determination to find her husband to feel curious. She waved toward the saloon. "Could you please go inside and see if my husband's there? If he is, please ask him to step outside for a few minutes to talk to me."

"Certainly, Mrs. Morgan."

Watching him disappear into the saloon, Prudence wondered what she'd do if Michael refused to come outside to her. She stiffened her spine. *I'll go in after him.*

But she didn't have to put her resolution into practice, for Mr. Phillips appeared in the doorway. "Rigsby hasn't seen head or tail of him."

Prudence frowned. "He said he was going to the pigpens. Could you tell me where they are?"

"Ah," he said, nodding. "Heard a piglet was stolen, which riled up the China men. The boss won't be happy." He pointed up the street. "Behind the tents."

"Thank you, Mr. Phillips."

"My pleasure, ma'am. I, um, wanted to say thank you for the party. I know it ended poorly. The men all felt badly about that, seeing you're new and all, and were all gussied up. I know you ladies worked hard. We had us a darn good time."

All day, Prudence had only been able to think of the party with shame, assuming she'd been an object of ridicule, both from Obadiah Kettering throwing up on her and her screams in reaction.

"Hope we can have us another one, without the bad ending. I promise we'll sit on Kettering all day so he doesn't have a chance at any liquor."

The idea made her smile. "I'll keep that in mind, Mr. Phillips." She nodded a dismissal. "If you'll excuse me, I need to find my husband."

Leaving the miner behind, Prudence strode up the street, her mind busy with what the man had said about a stolen pig.

How vile of Michael to make me think his errand to the pigpens was my fault when all along he'd planned to go there anyway.

Prudence was done with honeyed words. *Time to give my husband a piece of my mind.*

Chapter Eighteen

Michael stood next to the pigpens, trying not to show his impatience to finish the discussion and get to the saloon.

Hong Guan, who was the usual spokesperson for his compatriots, was dressed in his customary loose gray pants and tunic. He'd taken ages to describe the problem of the stolen piglet, mostly because distress made his broken English even more unintelligible. His emotion showed in the deepening crinkle of lines around his eyes and the way he gestured with his hands, when normally the man kept them still.

Michael knew the matter required delicate handling. The China men were among his best miners. He'd take a dozen more if he could, but recruiting them for this out-of-the-way town took some doing. The Orientals worked harder than most white men for less pay and caused very little trouble. Mostly, like today, the trouble came to them—a fact he'd done his best to prevent in Morgan's Crossing.

Only by putting his foot down on bullying did Michael maintain a shaky peace between the whites and the China men. He'd forbidden his white men from pulling the China men's pigtails or even threatening to chop them off. Nor did he allow beating of the Orientals.

Probably plenty of taunting went on out of his sight, but such was the way of the world. Men shuffled themselves into a hierarchy, often picking on the ones beneath them. Michael, at the top of the heap, mostly paid the jostling no mind, except at times like now, when he had to intervene. A piglet was valuable, making the loss keenly felt. That these men had roasted a piglet and brought it as a gift to his wedding party made Michael even more inclined to be sympathetic.

He surveyed the three different pigpens separated by low fences, each presided over by a sow and her litter, with the boar in a pen off to the side. The row of tents was just beyond the range of the stench, but he imagined that the kind of squeals a pig made when you picked one up would be heard. No sign of predator tracks were on the ground, which meant not an animal predator, but a human one had stolen it. Meanwhile, the muddy ground around and within the pens showed plenty of footprints. No way to trace whose were whose.

His jaw clenched. "I'll pay you for the pig, until we find out who did it, and then I'll dock the man's wages. To keep this from happening again, I'll spread the word that I'll fire the culprit or culprits if there's a second offence."

Hong bowed, smiled, and thanked Michael.

Good, I can finally get out of here.

The stench of the pigpens made him take shallow breaths. Michael desperately wanted another drink to drown his sorrows...or, more aptly, his angers. He promised himself that once he found the source of the problem, he'd head to Rigsby's and let alcohol smooth the edge off his ire. Maybe with a few drinks in him, he could better handle Prudence. *Nothing else I've tried has worked.*

"Michael!"

At the sound of his wife's voice, he stiffened. *Speak of the devil. Is there a word for female devil?* He couldn't think of one. He nodded good-bye to Hong and was stepping away when—

"Michael, I want to talk to you!" Her voice rose until the timbre was almost a shriek. She ploughed pell-mell for him, her face red with anger.

Hong ducked into his tent. Out of sight, maybe, but not out of earshot.

The Guans' should stuff cotton in their ears to block out the worst of Prudence's screeches.

"I need a drink," he said, beginning to turn away.

"Oh, dear Lord. Don't tell me you're a drunkard like that Obadiah Kettering. Is that another thing you omitted to tell me about your character?"

He swung back.

She stood inches away, arms flung wide.

"You omitted telling me I'd be marrying a shrew," he said. "You should have written the word at the top of your fancy stationary in *big block letters.*" He sketched the word in the air and stated each letter. "S-H-R-E-W!"

"Why...why I never!" Her mouth opened and closed as if she sought just the right words to hurl at him.

"As for being a drunkard. Up until today, I only occasionally sought refuge in the bottle. But I think being married to you, my dear wife, will make me a frequent patron of Rigsby's Saloon. In fact, I might as well take up residence in the place."

Stepping forward, she brought up her hand to slap him.

He leaped out of the way.

Prudence missed, and her hand sailed past, making her off balance.

Sure she was going to try again, Michael moved away, putting more space between them.

Prudence slipped on a slimy rock and lost her balance, rotating and stepping sideways only to catch her heel in the hem of her skirt. She teetered backward toward the pigpen. Her legs hit the low fence, catching her at knee-height.

Oh, no! Michael leaped to catch her.

With a horrified expression, Prudence windmilled her arms in an effort to right herself.

Michael missed, grabbing only a fold of her skirt. He yanked back, hoping to pull her upright, but instead, with a ripping sound, the fabric tore.

The momentum toppled Prudence backwards into the pigpen, where she landed on her rump in the mire. "Grrrrrr!" She scooped up two handfuls of mud and flung them at him.

Shocked, Michael didn't dodge until the last minute, and the stinking mud went splat against his chest and face.

Covered in embarrassment as thick as the filth on her clothing, Prudence stormed down the street toward her house, formulating plans for an escape from this detestable place. She was careful not to make eye contact with any of the astonished townsfolk, who'd stopped to stare at the spectacle of their first lady covered in mud and pig excrement, her skirt torn and white petticoat showing.

I'll have to ride one of Michael's horses. Her anger with her husband overrode a spurt of fear about traveling alone through the open wilderness. *I'll send for my trunks when I arrive in St. Louis. Where will I stay?*

I can't think about that now. I just need to leave here.

A huge wagon with a team of six mules pulled to a stop in front of her house. For a moment, she felt a pang of uncertainty. Michael was holed up in the saloon and not available to deal with the business, whether a delivery for the mine or the store.

As she approached the rig, a thought struck her. Perhaps she could call upon the driver to take her to Sweetwater Springs. *Surely the driver can be trusted…what is his name?* Prudence racked her brain but couldn't remember.

A wide-brimmed brown hat pulled low shadowed the driver's face. The man set the brake, tied off the reins, and swung down from the wagon, his caped black coat swirling around him. He gave a quick glance up the street before turning to her, lifted his hat in greeting, and then snugged it back on.

Probably can't wait to get to the saloon.

"El Davis," said the teamster. "Ma'am." The teamster was a slight man, not much bigger than Prudence, with an attractive narrow face, and a long, straight nose. His brown eyebrows slanted above sky blue eyes made more vivid by the navy-blue muffler wrapped around his neck and covering part of his chin. He wore his blond hair cropped short and, from what she could see of his lower face, was clean-shaven. If she had met him elsewhere, she would never have taken him for a teamster.

He eyed her bedraggled state, and his nostrils widened, obviously smelling the miasma of pig that clung to her dress and gloves. Amusement gleamed in his eyes.

At least he has the good manners not to comment. "You take freight to the towns around Sweetwater Springs, is that right, Mr. Davis?"

"At your service." He gave her a small bow. "Mrs. Morgan, I presume?" he echoed in a friendly tone.

"Yes." *But not for much longer.*

He turned and lifted a brown-paper parcel from the wagon seat. "This is for you and Mr. Morgan from Mrs. Walker." He started to deposit the parcel into her arms.

Prudence held up her hands to show him the mud on her gloves. *Mrs. Walker?* She had to think a moment before she realized he meant Darcy Russell. *How long ago my days at the agency seemed.*

"I'll just set this on the porch for you. I have the bed Mr. Morgan ordered for the guest room, in addition to other supplies. I've brought your trunks and barrel as well."

"Don't unload them yet, Mr. Davis. The thing is…I'm in a tight spot. I need you to take me to Sweetwater Springs right away. I can pay you."

"Ah, cain't do that, ma'am." He shook his head.

She didn't see the problem and was about to sharply say so when she caught herself. *Use honey, Prudence,* she cautioned herself. *You need to win him to your side.* "Of course you can, Mr. Davis," she said sweetly, batting her eyelashes. "Why, I see at a glance you're quite a capable driver."

"I don't take passengers," he said gruffly. "'Specially not ones of the female persuasion."

"Why ever not? There's plenty of room on that, that..." She waved toward the wagon. *Monstrosity.*

"It's my policy, ma'am, and I don't have to explain myself to anyone," the teamster said, his tone remaining even and firm.

Will nothing move this man? Prudence abandoned honey for begging. "Please, Mr. Davis. I'm desperate to leave this place!"

He held up a hand to forestall her. "I've had a long drive to get here, Mrs. Morgan. My mules are tired and hungry, and so am I."

She remembered Michael's uneaten dinner. "I can offer you some of Mrs. Tisdale's rabbit pie."

"That's mighty kind, ma'am. But even so, I'm *not* about to turn around and head into the night. I intend to sleep in my own bed. Besides, what would Mr. Morgan say to the idea of you traipsin' all over the country with me?"

"Mr. Morgan has no say in my doings whatsoever."

Mr. Davis cocked an eyebrow. "According to the law, he has a great deal of say over you."

She sputtered and tightened her hands.

His expression softened. "I don't agree with the law in cases where one or both parties want to dissolve the marriage." Once again, his gaze rested on her muddy outfit.

"You'll have to excuse my appearance, Mr. Davis. I've had quite a day," she rambled in embarrassment. *How can I even explain?* "First, I gave an impromptu reading lesson to one of the children, then beat off Clyde Rossmore with my parasol so I could help Mrs. Tisdale deliver Portia's baby, then—"

"What!" he exclaimed, urgency in his tone. "Is Portia well? The baby?"

The fear in his eyes told Prudence far more than she suspected the man might wish her to know. *He loves Portia. How tragic.*

The teamster turned, seemingly abandoning his team and wagon, to head up the street.

"Wait! Where are you going?"

"To see Portia and the baby."

She gasped in alarm and caught his arm. "You can't, Mr. Davis. I don't know if Mrs. Tisdale is still there attending her. Clyde will *kill* Portia if he hears a man visited her, especially unchaperoned. Or maybe he'll hurt the baby. If you *care* about Portia, Mr. Davis, as I suspect you do, as well as her sweet baby girl, you will *leave her be*." She enunciated the last words.

"A girl," he whispered, longing in his eyes.

"Lissa May. As beautiful as her mother."

In obvious despair, he put up a hand to hide his face, partially turning away, his shoulders slumping.

Prudence knew the haunted look of pain she'd glimpsed would stay with her for a long time. She couldn't imagine loving someone so deeply—not only knowing you couldn't have her, but living with the certainty of her misery and abuse. She squeezed his arm, trying to convey what meager support she could. "I'm so sorry."

The teamster dropped his hand and swallowed, pulling himself together. "If I stay here..." His fists clenched. He shook his head and squared his shoulders, seeming to arrive at a decision. "I'll see to the needs of my team while you pack," he said, his voice still hoarse with emotion."

"Thank you," Prudence said. "I have two more trunks to load." Just saying so made real the fact that she was leaving Michael, and her heart pinched.

"Howie can help me with the mules, unload the bed and supplies Mr. Morgan ordered, and bring down your other trunks." His gaze narrowed. "Will Mr. Morgan give you any trouble?"

"He'll be glad to see me go," she said, her bitter tone reflecting the pain she felt.

"Darkness will fall by the time we pull out of town but the moon's full enough that we can get a good start. We'll take it slow. The mules have already worked hard today."

His change of heart should have given her a huge sense of relief, but instead, Prudence felt only sadness. Somehow, in the last few minutes, her anger at Michael had seeped away. But not her resolve to leave Morgan's Crossing. "Thank you, Mr. Davis."

"We should reach the first shelter by midnight. I'll sleep in the wagon, though."

Prudence gave him a wan smile. "I know I'm perfectly safe with you, Mr. Davis." She turned and walked to the porch. She paused, deciding that muddy prints on the paper of the parcel wouldn't matter, so she picked it up, hefting the unexpected weight, and continued into the house, her steps as heavy as her heart.

She didn't stop at the study to put away her papers. Maybe later, she'd write Michael a letter informing him of the truth about the store and Mr. Hugely, and he could search her work for himself.

Once in her bedroom, she eyed her trunks. Since Mr. Davis was unloading a bed and other supplies, there should be room for them in his wagon. She set the parcel on her bed.

Darcy must have sent us a wedding gift. Prudence hadn't thought to take refuge with one of the other mail-order brides. But now she realized that might be the best plan—at least until she thought things through. *Oh, the irony.* She'd be away from her husband, but still close enough…She imagined Michael coming after her, falling to his knees, and begging her to return. *Of course, I'll spurn him….*

Somehow the daydream didn't give her the satisfaction it should have. Careful not to get her hands dirty, she peeled off her gloves, and then tore the paper off the parcel. There stood a stack of books bound with string. *How like Darcy to send us books,* Prudence thought with something almost akin to affection. She picked up the first book, thinking she might take one along to read. Tilting it to catch the fading light through the window, she read the title: *The Taming of the Shrew.*

With an angry gasp, Prudence threw the book on the bed. *Well, I certainly won't stay with Darcy. That leaves Lina.*

She bit her lip, not at all certain Lina would welcome her after Prudence had been so cruel to the Italian woman. *Lina has a kind heart. If I throw myself on her mercy, maybe she'll at least put me up for a few days.*

Prudence divested herself of the shirtwaist and skirt. Her handkerchief dropped to the ground. She threw the garments and her gloves into the corner. She leaned over to grab the handkerchief and wipe off her hands, and then picked up the broken parasol. She walked over to toss both on top of the heap.

She glanced down, checking to see if the mud had penetrated to her undergarments, but they remained white and dry. Luckily, the long tear in her dress was in the front, not the back.

Prudence removed her hat and unpinned her traveling dress and coat from the clothesline, grateful Mrs. Rivera had cleaned them. Quickly, she donned the clothing, switching out the purple hat for her traveling one. Mrs. Rivera had also stitched the stem of the errant daisy into place.

She touched the flower petal, realizing how some of the women in this town had come to mean so much to her. *May, Rosa, Portia, Cecelia.* She used their given names as if they were friends. *If I take nothing else from the wreckage of this marriage, I now know the importance of friendships—and even more, that I'm capable of forming them.*

Tears formed in her eyes. *Not now.* She sniffed them back, setting the hat on her head and tying the ribbons under her chin. With rapid movements, she began to pack, stopping halfway to light the lamp. When Prudence finished, she hurried downstairs carrying her satchel and the lamp.

El stood in the darkness of the kitchen, eating Michael's dinner.

"I'm ready." She set lamp on the counter and the satchel on the floor.

"Why don't you go wait in the wagon? Howie's hitching the team back up. When he comes in, we'll fetch your trunks and be off."

Prudence heard a tap at the backdoor. She turned, her heart jolting, hoping…. "Come in."

Howie entered, nodding and avoiding eye contact. He clearly wasn't happy at having to face Michael with the news that she'd left him.

"My trunks are upstairs."

Mr. Davis finished his food and handed her the plate and fork. He walked from the room, with Howie following to go upstairs.

As the sound of their boot heels faded, Prudence rinsed off the dishes and left them in the sink. Picking up her satchel, she slowly walked to the front doors. *To think only a few hours ago, I'd planned to fill this house—with furniture, with love—and make it a home.*

Prudence hadn't realized how important the dream of a new life with Michael had become, how her heart would ache as she passed through the two sets of doors.

Outside, dark had fallen, and a plump moon began the ascent into the velvet night sky, cutting a path through the sprinkling of stars. The wagon was turned, facing the opposite direction, the six pairs of mules already hitched. The one nearest her flicked an ear.

She reached up and deposited the satchel on the seat, then gathered the hem of her skirt and climbed aboard, grateful for the worn-leather cushion on the bench. She stared down the silent street. *Michael's in the saloon, and he doesn't know I'm leaving. Will he care?*

The two men came out of the house with her trunk and loaded it in the wagon. They went back inside and soon were out with the second.

El Davis climbed into the seat. He untied the reins, unlocked the brake, and reached for a bullwhip that lay on the seat next to him.

Howie stood in the dim light, somber-faced.

"Thank you, Howie," Prudence called.

This time, the stableman met her eyes. "Safe journey, ma'am," he said, his voice soft. He stepped back from the wagon and into the shadows.

With a smooth cast of his arm, Mr. Davis snapped the long whip over the head of the left lead mule. "Hi-ya!"

With a jolt, the wagon started.

Unable to resist the impulse, Prudence twisted to look behind her. The moonlight coated the gray boards of her house in silvery light, adding a magical aspect to her home. Throat tight, she bit her lip. *I've missed my chance at love.*

Prudence wanted to weep for how her dreams had crumbled to dust. But Mr. Davis was already beset by sorrow, so she held in her misery. She resolutely turned and set her face toward the wilderness.

Chapter Nineteen

Hunger finally drove Michael home from the saloon to face his wife. On the front porch a shadow detached and drifted over to him. In his relaxed state, he just glared at Howie. "Lucky, I don't shoot you."

"Ain't carryin' a gun," the man said in a low voice.

Michael grunted.

"Mrs. Morgan left with El Davis. Took all her trunks."

Must have heard wrong. Michael shook his head, trying to dislodge the cottony feeling in his ears. "What?"

"She's gone, boss."

Michael let out a curse and shoved passed Howie into the house.

"Don't let her get away," the stableman said in a low voice.

On the small table, a lamp glowed, and Michael moved toward it.

Wasn't like Howie to make suggestions. But then again, the man doesn't know the truth about Prudence.

Michael picked up the lamp and trotted up the stairs, down the hallway, and into the bedroom. He held up the lamp and slowly walked inside.

The bedroom was empty of most of Prudence's possessions, but the odor of the pigpen seeped from the muddied purple gown balled on the floor; a broken parasol, almost snapped in half, lay on top of the garment. A pile of books lay on her bed. She'd left no other items behind.

Michael moved closer to the bed, noting the title of the book on top, *The Taming of the Shrew.* He shook his head, wondering why she'd left it. *Probably because I kept calling her a shrew.* The thought made him ashamed.

His chest tight, Michael turned and walked out the door, moving downstairs, the sounds of his footsteps on the stairs echoing through the vacant house. He ignored the bed and crates piled in the parlor and moved into his study. Dropping into his desk chair, he stared blindly out the darkened window, realizing the home's emptiness corresponded with the cavity in his chest.

Dagnabbit, Prudence hasn't even lived here one week. Most of that time, I didn't even like her. I should be able to forget her in a matter of hours. I just need to put my mind to the task.

He sagged forward, pushing aside the account book for the store, and propping his elbows on the desk. On top of the open ledger, he noticed a paper scrawled with figures, different from her purchasing lists.

Puzzled, he picked up the sheet and studied the numbers—precise lines of figures. Some were labeled with store items laid out in a familiar manner. He read the comment about the freight fees written on the bottom.

He pulled the account book closer and laid the paper next to it. Sure enough, the rows lined up. It took a while of glancing back and forth between Prudence's work, the catalogue, and the ledger before comprehension dawned. Unlike Prudence, he was familiar with the items in the store, as well as the teamster's charges, and could discern the discrepancies in the accounts.

Michael grabbed the pen from the stand, dipped the tip in the inkwell, and laboriously added a few numbers of his own before reaching the same conclusion his wife apparently had. Hugely was jacking up the cost of the goods above the fifteen percent he was supposed to charge—more like thirty—but reporting only the lower percentage.

The realization, which normally would have catapulted Michael from his chair to go fire the shopkeeper and run him out of town, or maybe summon his mine guards to apprehend Hugely and deliver him to the sheriff in Sweetwater Springs, now was set aside for a larger problem—that of his runaway bride.

He'd wanted a buxom beauty to perform wifely duties and take a social role in his town. What he received was a plain termagant who, judging by these papers and the discovery that had taken her only hours to figure out, possessed superior intelligence and mathematical ability. He hadn't stipulated those qualities on his list for a wife, yet now knew he'd desperately needed them.

What have I done? Despair washed over him.

Michael took a long, hard look at his character and didn't like what he saw.

I called Prudence the shrew, but who was the one who jumped to conclusions without provocation? Me. Who'd been the first to turn mean today? I was.

Shame seized him. *I should not have married a woman I didn't want. Even so, when I vowed before God to love and cherish her, I should have kept my word—the word I claimed to be so proud of keeping. Yet I broke my vows.*

The ringing of the bell next to the outside doors startled him into sudden hope. *She's back.* But even as he thought the words, he knew Prudence would have no need to knock at the door of her own home. *No, she'd probably just barge in to rail at me.*

Michael pushed himself to his feet, moving slowly, as if his muscles ached. His body didn't hurt, but he was beginning to realize his heart might have taken a blow. *It's just my pride*, he assured himself, bracing for the gossip that was sure to come when his people learned his wife had fled. Mrs. Tisdale, here to deliver the meal, probably already knew.

The woman stepped inside, carrying her basket, accompanied by the smell of baked fish. She beamed at him. "Howie brought me the trout. Quite a good catch you had."

His morning's fishing expedition seemed like a lifetime ago.

Setting out the meal, Mrs. Tisdale inquired, "And how is Mrs. Morgan tonight? I heard about the argument at the pigpens." She tisked. "I can't believe you'd fight with her after what she'd done today." She shook her head in obvious admiration. "You should have seen your wife, Mr. Morgan. The way she took to Clyde Rossmore with that parasol of hers."

A few seconds passed as Michael tried to understand her words, so different from what he'd expected. "What—Rossmore?"

"Mrs. Morgan didn't tell you? Probably too modest. No wonder why you were fighting instead of giving her the respect she deserves." Mrs. Tisdale sent a pointed look at his shirt.

He'd wiped off the mud at the saloon and washed his hands and face, but the dried blotches remained.

"The baby is fine. I checked after I saw Clyde had left for the saloon."

"What?" Michael repeated, feeling at even more of a loss. "Portia Rossmore had her baby?"

She eyed him in puzzlement. "You haven't heard?"

He tried to control his irritation. "I've heard nothing." Probably because at the saloon, after Michael had downed a shot of whiskey at the bar to take the edge off his anger, he'd retreated to a dim table in the corner, nursing a glass. Later, when the miners trickled in, he glared at any who attempted to move in his direction, and they veered away. Aside from uttering "whiskey," he hadn't spoken a word all evening.

"When Mrs. Rossmore went into labor, that man of hers wouldn't let me in the door. I knew by the time I had summoned you to help, much could go wrong, so I fetched Mrs. Morgan instead. That brute wouldn't allow her in the house, either. But she wouldn't let that stop her. No, indeed. Not even when he raised his fists."

Michael's mouth opened and closed like a trout jerked out of the river and tossed onto land. Anger shot through him and he stood. "Clyde Rossmore laid hands on my wife?"

"Not a bit." Mrs. Tisdale said cheerfully. "When he

threatened to harm her, she broke her parasol over his head."
She laughed at the memory. "Right proud I was. Mrs. Morgan
threatened that *you* would punish him if he harmed her, and she
chased him off to the saloon so we could deliver the baby in
peace. Seemed quite certain of your protection."

"She was?" The thought warmed through his anger and
confusion. He sat down once more.

Mrs. Tisdale patted his arm. "*Quite* certain. Even after such a
short time, your wife has discerned your character."

"I'm afraid you're only too right," Michael said in a hollow
voice. "Mrs. Morgan has discerned my character and, thus, has
left me. We had an argument about this list of hers." He
pounded his fist on the papers. "Before the pigpen one. Stupidly
started by me."

"That's what apologies are for, Mr. Morgan. I've noticed you
hand them out sparingly as do many men."

He sighed and ran a hand over his head. "That will be
changing from here on out."

"Are you certain she's left?"

"El Davis took her back to Sweetwater Springs. Howie
confirmed it."

"Newlyweds." Mrs. Tisdale tisked. "I know all too well what
an adjustment the first weeks of marriage are."

Her matter-of-fact acceptance caught Michael off guard.
"You do?"

"Didn't I up and go to my parents' house after I was only
three days wed? A silly quarrel, really. I was home the next
morning. And Mr. Tisdale and I had known each other all
our lives—not like you and Mrs. Morgan." She gave a decisive
nod. "If I may?" She arched an eyebrow and pointed to the
papers.

Michael nodded permission. He rose and began to pace.

She picked one up, squinted, and held the paper an arm's
distance away. Her forehead wrinkled, and, as she read, Mrs.
Tisdale silently mouthed every word before lowering her arm
and looking at him. "I must admit, I don't know all of the words,

but what I do know seems quite reasonable to me. After all, your house is quite bare."

"What!" He couldn't believe practical Mrs. Tisdale would take Prudence's side. "Some furniture and things for the kitchen, supplies and such, yes. But bolts of material and lace? All kinds of mirrors? What need has she for all of that?"

Mrs. Tisdale gave him a glance as sharp as one of the earlier ones from Prudence. "She doesn't. *We* do. The ladies of Morgan's Crossing."

"So then...she...?"

The woman lowered the paper and tapped a line dividing the columns in half. "Mrs. Morgan is placing an order for the store. She's seeing to the needs of the womenfolk and children of this town."

Michael couldn't have been more shocked if she'd hit him with a pickaxe. He shook his head in dismay. "The children? The ladies?"

"When she toured the store, Mrs. Morgan was quite concerned about the lack of merchandise."

"I've wronged her." In despair, he sank into a chair. "I don't know what to do now."

Mrs. Tisdale dropped a comforting hand on his shoulder and squeezed. "Yes, you do, Mr. Morgan." she said in brisk accents. "You just need to search your heart. And I'll leave you to do your thinking."

"Mrs. Morgan's muddy, torn gown is upstairs. Do you think Mrs. Rivera can save the dress?"

"Your poor wife." Mrs. Tisdale shook her head. "She's had quite a day. No wonder she's run away." She gave him an approving nod. "Good to think in terms of your wife returning. I'll send Mrs. Rivera for the clothing later. But nothing will repair that parasol of hers. You're going to have to send for a new one." She wagged a finger at him. "But first, mind you, eat your victuals. A man's got to keep up his strength at a time like this." With that parting shot, Mrs. Tisdale left.

Following her command he ate the food, his eyes on the

ledgers. The baked trout might as well have been mush for all the attention he paid, and Michael didn't even notice how he'd consumed the bread without any butter or jam.

After he'd finished, Michael let out a long sigh and sat back in his chair, pondering his options. The most obvious one was to let Prudence go and seek an annulment. Marry another woman, one more suited to him—travel to a town to find her. The other was to go after his wife and force her to return. *Is that what I want?* Michael wasn't sure.

Feeling conflicted, he gazed at the ledgers and realized what he really wanted was to become better acquainted with his wife and she with him. *Perhaps if I stopped looking at her through the window of unmet expectations and appreciated the unique qualities she does have….*

The memory came to him of the day he'd written the letter for a mail-order bride. He'd been thinking of the plight of Portia Rossmore and wanted a woman with a backbone who'd wallop him with a frying pan if need be. *Well, turns out I received the kind of wife I wished for.*

A chill raised the fine hairs at the nape of his neck, and he realized that perhaps Divine Intervention was at play in his marriage. Perhaps God had chosen the very wife for Michael that he *needed*, rather than giving him what he *wanted*. *I certainly haven't suffered any tedium since her arrival. She's brought me plenty of problems, my Pru has, but boredom isn't one of them.*

Maybe she'd make me a better wife than the one I thought I wanted. He tapped a finger on her sheets of paper, wondering if Prudence would be willing to take on the bookkeeping, which would certainly free up his time to give her his attention in the evenings.

I'll never know unless we try. He surged to his feet.

I could ask her to come back and give our marriage a chance. If she still doesn't want to stay with me, I'll drive her to Sweetwater Springs and put her on the train myself.

Enjoying the sunny day—for Gideon had warned her the weather could turn any time now—Darcy strode down the path through the forest on her way to the mail-and-supply boxes, situated on the road to Sweetwater Springs. The loamy ground under her feet was still spongy from yesterday's rain. Even after living here for six weeks and walking this path almost daily, she still spotted new wonders in the forest, such as the dragonfly flitting over a clump of asters to land on one purple flower.

She reached the sloping-roofed shelter. Gideon had built the shallow structure with carved wooden boxes on both sides, so Jonah Barrett, any of the Dunns, or their ranch hands could deposit mail and supplies in their travels back from town. Not that the Walkers needed the help anymore since they attended church regularly. But receiving mail delivered by a neighbor was nice, rather than having to wait until Sundays.

A smile played about Darcy's lips. While Gideon would probably always have a solitary nature—and, indeed, she wouldn't want him any other way—she was so proud of the changes in him. In order to protect her, he'd faced his fears of mixing with society, managing the trip to Sweetwater Springs on Sundays. With the expansion of his circle of friends from just their closest neighbor, Jonah, she knew her husband had come to enjoy spending time with the other men.

I'm so blessed. After she'd deliberately chosen spinsterhood to pursue her intellectual interests and avoid suitors only courting her for her wealth, Darcy had unexpectedly forged a rare and deep union with Gideon. She savored every day with her beloved husband.

Darcy reached the mailbox, lifted the lid, and with joy spied a letter within. She pulled out the envelope, thrilled to see Kathryn's familiar handwriting. Tearing open the envelope, she pulled out two pages and turned toward home, reading as she walked.

Y Knot, Montana Territory

Darcy, no! Pru so close to Sweetwater Springs is a punishment none of you deserve! I'm speechless, to say the least. I can't imagine this horrible turn of events, although I can easily see you tossing out Prudence's name to that atrocious Mr. Morgan as if the sound was sweet on your tongue, all the while crossing your fingers behind your back. I must confess, the thought of that moment does make me smile.

Good ol' Pru married, and within a two-day ride of you and the other brides—that's just not right. I remember counting the days until I didn't have to wake up to her sour face scowling from across the breakfast table at the bride agency as I ate my toast and marmalade, her mind always spinning ways to spoil my day as well as everyone else's. Poor Trudy, poor Lina, poor you! I was sitting out back snapping peas when my dearest Tobit brought me your letter. When I gasped, he suspected the worst, thinking something horrible had happened to one of my friends in Sweetwater Springs. He just doesn't understand when I describe her manipulating and hurtful ways, but that is because he is so kind, affectionate, and perfect.

Well, enough about Pru. Thinking about her makes me want to take to the hayfields where I can whack to my heart's delight. (Yes, I said hayfields. Scything is just one of the many things I've learned since becoming Mrs. Tobit Preece.) I will keep you all in my prayers, as I always do, and pray she finds the voyage to your peaceful town too arduous. Perhaps you won't have to suffer her razor-sharp tongue but a few times a year.

You will be happy to hear I have no ill effects leftover from my bout with amnesia, except for a tiny headache now and then. Dr. Handerhoosen assures me those will diminish as time goes on.

I have indeed learned to can vegetables and fruits, but not from Heather or Mrs. Klinkner, that saint of a woman, but from Isaiah, Tobit's grandfather. I'm sure you remember how suspicious he was of me when I first came to the farm. His comments had me in tears more than once. Well, since Isaiah walked me down the aisle to marry his grandson, he's a changed man, and I love him dearly. He's my most ardent ally, after Tobit, of course.

The three of us spent a week in the kitchen getting the last of the vegetables put up, as well as the first apples of the season. They're both such hard workers, they would put men I knew from my old life to shame. (Oscar, the scoundrel, would be at the top of that list!) At first, I just helped and watched, but I caught on quickly and even put up a batch of tomatoes myself. I have big news here! Do you remember Heather's younger sister Sally? Unbeknownst to anyone here, she set out for Y Knot to surprise her siblings. When the stagecoach she was traveling in had an accident, she was the only one able to ride for help. I can hardly believe she was so brave to set out alone, bareback on a mule. On the way, snow began to fall, and she got lost. By God's good grace, she stumbled upon a cabin somewhere in the mountains. All of us shudder when we think of what could have happened. Well, as astonishing that this sounds, she was found by one of our good friends, Roady Guthrie.

Tomorrow night is our harvest social, and I'll get to speak with her myself—and find out all the details. I've yet to meet her. I hear she is a sweet thing, but how could she be anything else with Heather for a sister?

Evie is well. She and Chance are just so lovely together. They are preparing for the coming birth with great excitement. Heather and Hayden are very well, too, although I know how much Heather pines to become in the family way. I tell her to pray for patience, and not to worry, but sometimes there is just that certain look behind her eyes that makes me stop and give her a hug. Out here on this fertile farm I see the wonder of new life every day, which makes me anticipate the day I can write and tell you I'm expecting, too.

I'm delighted to hear about your days filled with love and happiness. The more you write me of your marriage, the more perfect the match between you and Gideon sounds.

Send my love to Trudy and Lina. Tell them they are missed and loved. I'll tell the girls here to write more often. I think they've just been so busy with their new lives.

About your other questions, I hardly have time to play the piano for pleasure, let alone taking on students. Perhaps in a year or two. I love the farm, the animals, the clean air, and yes, the work. This life suits me better than I'd thought possible. I'm working on getting Mother, Father, and Poppy to come meet Tobit and Isaiah. I'd love to show them around Y Knot. I know they'd be shocked at how primitive the town is, but I wouldn't change a thing.

Sending you all my love,
Kathryn Preece

Darcy moved from the forest through the arching trellis made from the interwoven branches of two sentinel trees and vines and onto the flagstone pathway. She stopped, as had become her routine, to admire her new house—a fairy-tale cottage with a large square turret, rebuilt after the fire set by her half-brother. Just yesterday, Gideon had painted the arch-shaped door a forest green, which contrasted with the unweathered wood of the squared-off logs. The stacked stone flowerbeds lining the walkway and around the house were empty, cleared of the foliage that was charred in the blaze. The reminder of their close escape from death served to fill her with gratitude for their survival.

Today, Darcy tried to see the place through Prudence's eyes—not that she could imagine the virago ever visiting, thank goodness. She'd never seen any sign of the unpleasant woman having a whimsical nature, so the charm of her and Gideon's dwelling would be lost on Prudence. *All the poorer for her.*

She hurried down the flagstone path to Gideon's workshop, where the windows and door stood open, and paused in the entrance, inhaling the smell of cedar sawdust. The room seemed larger now that so much of the furniture he'd lovingly crafted over the years had been moved into the house.

Gideon bent over a hope chest, sanding the surface. His hair, such a pale blond that it seemed white, had grown longer since they'd met, and now he wore it tied back in a tail, like a hero of old. He looked up and smiled.

The warmth in his silvery eyes made her stomach tingle. Darcy waved the letter and stepped to his side. "I've heard from Kathryn. She's happy in her marriage, and her memory continues to improve." Saying the words gave her such a pang of missing her dear friend. "If you don't need me, I want to visit Lina and share the news. I'll stay a while to visit and play with Adam."

"You know I always need you," Gideon said with a sweet smile, brushing a hand over the surface of the cabinet. "I'll go along. Jonah mentioned on Sunday about needing my help on a section of their fence that's fallen down." His eyes twinkled. "Bet Lina will make us some pasta and red sauce." He wiped his palm on his leg. "Any other news from Y Knot?"

"Kathryn was properly sympathetic about Prudence moving to our area. I'll tell you the rest on the way to the Barretts'." Still disturbed by thoughts of Prudence, Darcy moved closer to her husband. "I just know that woman is going to be a problem."

Gideon raised an eyebrow, crinkling his forehead. "So far she hasn't been," he chided in a gentle tone. "'Never let the future disturb you. You will meet it, if you have to, with the same weapons of reason which today arm you against the present.'"

"Marcus Aurelius." Darcy leaned against him, taking a breath of the cedar-scented air and allowing herself to relax. "There's only one consolation," she said. "Morgan's Crossing is miles from here, and I doubt we'll ever see that woman. At least, Prudence Crawford Morgan can't do anything to disturb our peace."

Chapter Twenty

The smell of the tomato-rich minestrone soup hung in the air. Darcy lingered in the doorway of the Barrett house, watching Lina sweep the porch.

Lina looked up. "Well?"

"Adam went down like a lamb. I do believe Auntie Darcy has developed the magic touch."

"Thank goodness for that. He's refused to nap during the last few days." She threw up a hand. "*Madonna Mia.* I adore my Adam, but that boy can wear me out. So I'm grateful you turned the tables and wore *him* out."

Darcy stepped onto the porch. "You know how much Adam fascinates me. I was never around children. So he's a new creature for me to study," she said in a teasing tone. "I'll play with him every chance I can." She looked across the field to where Jonah and Gideon were rebuilding the fence. "Looks like the men are halfway through."

Lina followed her gaze. "We'd better get supper started. I was thinking something simple. Pasta and red sauce. Minestrone, too, of course. Perhaps, we'll make biscuits and use the huckleberry jam we made."

"I have no problem with that. You know how much Gideon

loves your red sauce. I think he just trailed along today in hopes you'd cook some."

Lina chuckled. "I've said I could teach you how to make it."

"And give up Gideon's favorite excuse for visiting? Do you really want to see less of me?" Darcy saw movement in the distance. "Someone's coming." She moved to the rail and shaded her eyes against the sun.

Lina stepped to her side. "Looks like that teamster, El Davis. I saw him go by a few days ago after picking up the package you sent to Prudence."

"Why is he returning this way, instead of taking the main road?"

Lina poked Darcy's side with her elbow. "Prudence probably sent back your *gift*," she teased.

Darcy chuckled, leaning forward. "That's quite an equipage he has there. Six mules."

"He's slowing," Lina said in a puzzled tone. "That's strange. We haven't ordered anything."

"Wrong direction, even if you did. He's coming from Morgan's Crossing, not Sweetwater Springs. Looks like a woman is with him."

The huge wagon rolled to a stop, but the barn blocked their view of the road, so they did not see who alighted. Soon, however, a woman appeared, walking up the dirt drive to the house. Something was familiar about the way she moved."

A frisson ran down Darcy's spine.

Lina stiffened. She reached out and grabbed Darcy's arm. "*Prudence!*" she hissed. "What's *she* doing here?"

Jonah and Gideon cut across the field, probably to help the driver unhitch the mules to drink at the horse trough.

"This is *not* good." Darcy thought of her sensitive husband, who'd suffered so much abuse at the hands of his mother. Her protective hackles rose. *If I hear Prudence say one critical word to him, I'll scratch her eyes out!* "I knew she'd find a way to make trouble."

"Trouble is definitely walking up my driveway." Lina turned

to her, an uneasy look in her brown eyes. "What do we do, Darcy? What if she's mean to Adam?"

"He's sleeping." Darcy's stomach clenched, and she tried not to show her concern. Adam would be the perfect target for Prudence's meanness. The woman would never see the child's sweetness, his intelligence, his quicksilver personality. Instead, she'd only judge the toddler for being a half-breed. "Surely even Prudence Crawford wouldn't sink so low," Darcy said, not at all convinced. "We'll talk on the porch. That way if she turns nasty, we'll just go inside and shut the door in her face. Adam will never know."

Prudence drew closer. She was dressed in an unbecoming traveling coat, not unlike the one Darcy had worn on her own trip to Sweetwater Springs. A flowered straw hat shaded her face. Although she held her head high, their nemesis wasn't wearing her customary smirk. Instead, she looked sad, maybe even vulnerable.

Wishful thinking, Darcy chided herself. *Don't let down your guard.*

"Maybe we should get the rifle, just in case," Lina muttered, shaking her head.

Darcy nudged her friend with her hip. "You have the broom. Start with that. The rifle will be our fall back weapon."

Both Lina and Darcy! Prudence hadn't expected the two to be together. *This encounter will be twice as hard.*

The closer Prudence came to the two women standing on the porch, the more nervousness churned in her stomach. Her steps faltered. *This is a bad idea. I should have gone straight to Sweetwater Springs instead of coming here. But the damage is done.*

Looking at the implacable expressions of her fellow mail-order brides made Prudence want to turn and flee, but pride wouldn't allow a retreat. Instead she lifted her chin and quickened her pace, striding up the steps of the porch as if she belonged there. "Good morning, Darcy, Lina." *Is it still morning?*

She had no idea of the time. Not ready to reveal her plight, she simply said, "I've come to pay a call."

Darcy watched her with cold gray eyes. She glanced from the men leading the mules to the trough and back to Prudence. "You came all the way from Morgan's Crossing in that wagon to *pay a call?*"

Prudence lifted an eyebrow. "Why, yes," she said tartly. "Isn't that why you're here, too? Paying a call on Lina?" *Oh, dear Lord, I've done it again. Use honey, Prudence.* She forced herself to soften her tone and glanced at Lina. "I was looking forward to some of your minestrone soup."

Lina's eyes sparked, and she drew herself up.

Oh, dear. She thinks I'm being sarcastic.

"You are welcome here, Prudence. However—" Lina shook her finger under Prudence's nose, her cheeks flushed, corkscrew curls flying. "If you say *one* nasty word to my husband or son— show either of them any disrespect—I will revoke my hospitality, as much as it goes against my notion of what is right," she said, her Italian accent thick.

"Or do so to Gideon, either," Darcy interjected.

Lina fisted her hands on her plump hips. "I'll chase you out of here with my broom, Prudence Crawford, like the witch you are. I swear this before the Blessed Virgin!"

"Morgan," Prudence corrected, her temper rising. She tried to hide how stunned she was by Lina's transformation into a protective harridan. "Prudence *Morgan*. Remember you recommended me to him? Mrs. Michael Morgan." She used her usual snide tone with Lina, even though she couldn't help feeling some grudging respect for her. "And if you're wielding the broom, then which of us is the witch?"

Although she'd flung the words in order to strike back at Lina, Prudence knew her ire wasn't really caused by her fellow mail-order bride, but because of a jealous wish that she cared about Michael's well-being as much as Lina did for Jonah's, and Darcy for Gideon's. *Why couldn't my match have turned out like theirs?*

Lina's eyes shot daggers, but Darcy's gaze chilled to ice. "I suggest you leave, *Mrs. Morgan,"* she said in an autocratic Boston accent. "You've just worn out your welcome."

Suddenly exhausted to her bones, Prudence held up a placating hand and gave Lina a sincere glance. "I truly wasn't ridiculing your minestrone. Your soup really is a favorite of mine. I just never told you. In fact, after you jumped off West, I made minestrone several times at the agency."

Lina's eyes widened.

Prudence pressed her lips together. Never before had she apologized for her behavior. "I'm *sorry*. I didn't mean to call you a witch. If truth be told, *I'm* the witch, not you." Her gaze swung to Darcy. "Not either of you."

Her apology hung in the air.

The stunned expression on the two women's faces made her quirk her lips in a small smile that disappeared the moment Prudence remembered why she was here. "And I didn't really come to pay a call. I've left my husband and have come to throw myself on your mercy."

Chapter Twenty-one

Feeling shocked at the apology but nonetheless intending to remain on her guard, Darcy exchanged a glance with Lina. A wordless communication passed between them, and they stepped back.

A relieved expression crossed Prudence's face, and her shoulders relaxed.

Lina waved her into the house. "Please come inside, Mrs. Morgan," she said in a formal tone.

After they entered, Darcy watched Prudence like a hawk eying a rat, waiting to see a familiar sneer. *Will Prudence scorn Lina's humble abode? Or will she see past the small space, the simple furnishings—except for the bedroom set carved with Indian symbols Gideon had made—to the warmth that permeates the main room?*

Lina pointed to a rack. "You can hang your coat and hat there."

Prudence gave a quick glance around to the kitchen on the left and parlor area on the right, her expression remaining pleasant. "How cozy," she said without a trace of condescension. "And I can smell the minestrone simmering." She undid the buttons on her coat. "I'm sure it wasn't so nice before you arrived, Lina." She hung up her coat and hat.

Has the world turned upside down? Darcy wondered.

Lina's expression softened. "A woman's touch was needed." She gestured to the stove. "I'll put the kettle on for tea. We can talk for a few minutes, but then Darcy and I need to prepare dinner."

"I can help," Prudence said with an eager tone. She smoothed down her dress, a plain blue one.

The offer, more than anything the woman had said so far, made Darcy suspect their fellow mail-order bride might very well have changed. The old Prudence would *never* have offered to cook. In fact, she'd avoided all domestic chores whenever possible.

Darcy decided to relax her guard and enjoy the company of the women. *At least until Adam wakes up and the men come inside.*

Lina moved to the stove and added wood. "Not much to do for the meal." She tapped the lid of the minestrone pot. "Soup's simmering." She moved the kettle of hot water to the center of the stovetop. "I just need to boil the pasta. I have red sauce already made in the icebox that needs to be heated. I intended to have Darcy shell some peas."

"What about biscuits?" Darcy reminded her friend.

"I can make those," Prudence interjected. Her expression turned wry. "You'll never guess how many batches I made after you left, Darcy. Dona was *determined* to make me into a baker."

Lina gave her an approving smile. "Then you shall, Prudence. Just know that my oven heats differently from the one at the agency, to my dismay. You'll need to turn the tray of biscuits several times so they don't burn." She pursed her lips. "But first, ladies, we shall renew our acquaintance. Darcy, dear, could you please pour the tea?"

"Certainly." She moved into the kitchen and took down three tin cups from a cupboard.

Lina dragged a chair from the kitchen table over to the two worn leather ones in front of the stone hearth and sat.

Prudence did likewise.

Darcy brought the mugs of steaming tea and set them on a round, marble-topped table—a gift from Trudy. She perched on the other leather chair and sent as warm a gaze as she could muster toward Prudence. "Now then, perhaps you should start from the beginning."

Prudence took a deep breath and described Mrs. Seymour's decision to temporarily close the agency, then the receipt of Mr. Morgan's letter, and her acceptance of his proposal. She detailed her travels and arrival in Sweetwater Springs, her voice wavering when she described sensing Michael's disappointment with her appearance. "I felt so hurt," she said in a soft voice.

Listening to Prudence admitting vulnerability made a pit grow in Darcy's stomach. *This is my fault.*

Prudence's voice strengthened when she described meeting the Nortons. "I'd never experienced kindness like Mrs. Norton's before. She made such an impression on me. Well," she amended, "I was more keenly *aware* of the kindness than ever before, I must admit."

"She's a wonderful woman." Lina nodded. "They are both really good people." They sipped tea, and Lina gestured with her mug. "It's not china like you're used to."

"Don't," Prudence snapped. "*Don't* apologize. China teacups don't matter, Lina. *Love* does." Her expression crumpled, and she burst into tears, covering her face with her hands.

"Oh, dear." Lina gave Darcy a helpless gaze. She rose and set down her cup on the end table. She moved her chair to Prudence's side, patting her hand. "There, there, now."

Shocked, Darcy remained frozen in place.

Prudence pulled a handkerchief from her sleeve and wiped her eyes. "I'm sorry. I don't mean to be a watering pot." But the tears didn't stop, and she cried and haltingly told them the rest of the story.

Darcy had never felt so guilty in her life. She scooted her chair closer. "I'm so sorry, Prudence. I'm the one who pointed Mr. Morgan in your direction. He set my back up, and I must admit, to my shame, I thought the two of you deserved each other. I acted maliciously."

"You spoke *truthfully*, Darcy." Prudence said, not meeting her eyes.

Darcy shook her head, determined to confess all. "I had ill intent toward you and Mr. Morgan."

Lina frowned. "Darcy, you must not take full responsibility. I participated, as did Trudy. We are all to blame for this predicament. I'm so very sorry, Prudence."

"Don't be." Prudence looked up and met their eyes. "For I'm not." Her eyes and nose were red and her cheeks splotchy, but the softness in her gaze and the strength in her tone made her look rather beautiful.

Darcy waited, sensing the woman wasn't finished.

"I don't know what is to come of me, but I will never be the same." Prudence dipped her chin and twisted her handkerchief. "What I've lived through in the last few days I will take with me always, regardless of where I go." She pressed a hand to her chest. "My heart is hurting for I felt this longing for Michael—feelings I've never had. They overpowered me in the strangest way."

Lina leaned forward. "My dear Prudence," she said with a kind smile. "You've fallen in love with your husband already."

"Love?" Prudence wrinkled her forehead in confusion. Her countenance cleared. "Very well, I love the man, or at least the man I *believe* Michael could be. I'm a better person because of my time in Morgan's Crossing and the people I met there." She sighed. "I can only be thankful."

Tears welled in Darcy's eyes. "You're a miracle, Prudence," she whispered through a tight throat.

Lina crossed herself. "I've been praying to the Blessed Mother for you, Prudence. But I must admit, I didn't do so until I'd heard you'd married Mr. Morgan. Jonah told us what that mining camp is like, and I've been worried."

At times like these, Darcy wished she had Lina's easy comfort and communication with the Divine. She gave thanks every day for her blessings but hadn't thought to pray for Prudence. *I will do so in the future.*

Darcy touched Prudence's knee. "In the words of William Butler Yeats, 'Every trial endured and weathered in the right spirit makes a soul nobler and stronger than it was before.'"

Prudence gave a shaky laugh. "Trust you, Darcy, to find a quotation at such a time as this."

"A quotation exists for *every* time," Darcy responded with conviction. "Now, Prudence, tell us the rest. I'm sure there's a great deal more to your story."

Prudence described her arrival in Morgan's Crossing and her unfavorable reaction to the town and her event-filled next two days, ending with her fight with Michael.

Darcy shook her head and let out the breath she'd been holding during Prudence's exciting narrative. "Well, you've had quite an adventure. Now that you've told us everything and had a good cry, we need to strategize. From your account, I don't think your marriage is hopeless." Raising an eyebrow, she looked at Lina to see if her friend concurred.

Lina nodded. "I agree."

"You just need a chance to talk things through—*calmly*. If Mr. Morgan truly cares for you, he'll be on Lina's doorstep soon."

Prudence sniffed and pressed the handkerchief to her nose. "What if Michael doesn't come?"

"Well, then, maybe you'll have to go to him, or you'll write to him. But no sense worrying now...."

"Not another quote." Lina made a mock expression of disapproval.

Darcy chuckled. "We'll cross that bridge *only* if we come to it."

At the fork in the road leading to Sweetwater Springs, something pricked through Michael's exhausted state and made him pull on the team's reins, bringing his wagon to a halt. This area must have experienced rain in the past few days, for some of the ruts were still muddy. Instead of heading straight along the road, the tracks of El Davis's wagon veered toward the right.

The Barretts live in that direction. And the Walkers.

Prudence has gone to her friends. What does she mean by that?

Maybe she's not as set on leaving as I thought. Sudden hope made him almost lightheaded in relief, for Michael knew if his wife had truly wanted to shake off the dust from their marriage, she'd have high-tailed it straight for the train station.

He flicked the reins, starting the horses and following the wagon's trail. As he drove, Michael thought through what he'd heard of the area, for he'd never driven this way before.

He knew most of the road passed through unsettled wilderness until the outskirts of Sweetwater Springs, with the Dunn ranch being the biggest spread out this way. But he wasn't too familiar with what lay to the right besides a few farms, among them the Barretts' and the Walkers'. The gossip about the mail-order brides had included only a few facts about their abodes. From rumor, he knew Gideon Walker's place was situated in the midst of the forest and not in view from the road. He recalled no details about the location of the Barrett place. *I'll have to watch the tracks carefully lest I miss a turnout.*

As he drove, Michael pondered what he'd say to Prudence to convince her to give him another chance. To his shame, since his marriage, he'd focused on getting his wife into his bed instead of learning about her and establishing a strong foundation for their future.

I'll apologize...and explain. I won't try to touch her, although I long to. Instead I'll do everything I can to make Prudence feel comfortable. To make her understand how much I need her—the town needs her.

Michael had never been much of a praying man, but now he beseeched the Good Lord for a second chance. The thought came that he might be praying for the wrong outcome. He mulled that over for a moment and switched to a different petition—one that probably was key to everything else. *Dear Lord, help me be a better man.*

Seeing the edge of a cultivated field surrounded by a railed fence, he sat upright, glancing between the field and the tracks he was following. He could see a barn near the road, a horse corral, and a house set farther in. A drive led to the house.

Two men worked together to mend a broken section of fence.

Both stood and watched him. Jonah Barrett and Gideon Walker. Jonah saluted as he drove by. "Morgan," he called in greeting.

I've come to the right place.

When passing the barn, Michael noticed the changes in the mule prints. Instead of the steady track they'd previously made, here they milled around, as if the driver had stopped. He turned the horses into the dirt drive.

On the porch sat a woman, and even from this distance, he recognized Prudence wearing a blue dress. His heartbeat kicked up, and he reined-in before a house that looked about three times as big as his miners' cabins, which wasn't saying much.

Prudence glanced in his direction.

He released a sigh that seemed dredged from his very depths, as if his chest had been too tight for him to breathe since he'd learned she'd left. *Thank you, God, that she's safe.* He hadn't realized he cared so deeply for her.

He set the brake, tied up the reins, and climbed down, walking to the porch, his eyes never leaving his wife.

Prudence sat on a bench, stirring something in a bowl with a wooden spoon. She gazed at him with a wary expression. Her nose and eyes were red, as if she'd been crying.

At least she hasn't run from me. Slowly, lest he scare her into the house, Michael set one foot on the porch, paused and leaned forward, placing an elbow on his knee. "Afternoon, Prudence. What are you doing?"

Prudence looked down at the bowl on her lap. "An experiment. You'll think I'm being silly."

He stayed silent, raising his eyebrows in encouragement for her to continue.

"Dona, the cook at the agency, told me that I needed to add love to the recipe when I bake. I thought she was being ridiculous, and she made me so angry." Prudence tilted her head toward the house. "In watching Lina cook, I realized Dona might be right."

Michael gave her a tender smile. "That's probably why Mrs. Tisdale's food tastes better than Cookie Gabellini's."

Prudence laughed. "I think there are many reasons Mrs. Tisdale's food tastes better." Her expression sobered, and she rose. "We have a lot to talk about, Michael. But I'm helping prepare the meal." She used her chin to gesture to the men working on the fence. "Go introduce yourself to Jonah and Gideon, and then take care of your team. I'm sure Lina won't mind if you stay for dinner."

That's my Pru taking charge.

He stepped fully onto the porch. "Thank you for being willing to talk to me, Prudence. I have much to hear, much to apologize for, and much to say. I know I've made a lot of mistakes and have come to make amends."

She reached up as if to touch him. "*We've* made a lot of mistakes." She lowered her hand.

"That we have."

Prudence turned toward the door. Then she paused and said over her shoulder, "There might be hope for us, after all."

After she'd gone inside, Michael stood still a moment, breathing out another prayer of thanksgiving. *Things aren't fixed yet, but she'd said there might be hope.* He trotted down the stairs, feeling as though he could dance a jig. With jaunty steps, he moved to meet two other men who'd married mail-order brides. *Bet they have interesting stories and valuable advice.* With the stakes so high, he was of a mind to listen.

Chapter Twenty-two

Platters of food were set on the red-and-white-checked tablecloth with Prudence's plate of golden biscuits taking pride of place in the center. Along one side, Jonah had rigged up a bench seat with some boards and wooden crates, so there'd be enough places for everyone.

The fragrance of red sauce and minestrone made Prudence's stomach grumble. She'd eaten a mouthful of beans at the wayfarer's shelter the previous night, and nothing before or since. But she was as nervous as she was hungry, wondering what everyone would think of her biscuits, *and* even more importantly, if everyone would get along.

Lina sat at the foot of the table, with Adam next to her in a high chair, Jonah at the head, and Darcy and Gideon across from Michael and Prudence. The Barretts said a blessing in Italian, with Adam chiming in on some of the words.

While the others prayed, Prudence kept her eyes open, wanting to absorb every nuance of this special meal—the first she'd ever eaten with people who might become friends. She glanced at the toddler, who banged a spoon on the table. Adam had his father's green eyes and the straight dark hair of his Indian mother. She'd taken one look at the adorable boy and had fallen in love.

Jonah passed around the platters of food, and Lina encouraged everyone to take generous helpings.

Darcy was the first to butter a biscuit and take a bite.

Feeling on tenterhooks, Prudence squeezed her hands together, waiting for the woman's reaction.

Darcy smiled, met her eyes, and nodded in obvious approval. "They're good, Prudence. Almost as good as Bertha's."

Lina chuckled. "That's high praise, indeed."

Prudence sucked in a sharp breath. *Still second best.* Familiar anger began to burn in her chest. She opened her mouth to retort, then clamped her teeth together, determined not to snap at Darcy. Instead, she took a breath. "Well, Bertha's are the best," she agreed in an amicable tone.

Lina gave her a sideways look, as if assessing the sincerity of Prudence's reaction, and then glanced at Darcy as if in confirmation.

They will take a while to feel as comfortable with me as they do with each other. To be fair, Prudence knew she might need a long time to believe in her own changes. *I'll constantly have to be on guard until I feel confident I can handle any situation with aplomb.*

Michael flourished his biscuit, as if giving Prudence a toast. His gaze rested on her with obvious pride. "I have no knowledge of Bertha and don't much care. But I will say I've never eaten better."

Prudence flushed with pleasure, placing a hand on her throat and keeping her eyes on his. "Really?"

"Not even my own mother's can match them, my dear."

Darcy spread jam on another piece. "I was just teasing you about your biscuits, Prudence. I really do think they're as good as Bertha's, and certainly better than mine."

Tears pricked Prudence's eyes. "That means a lot to me."

Michael's gaze cut to Darcy. "Mrs. Walker, you did me an unexpected service when you matched me with my wife." He winked at Prudence. "Took me a while, though, to see her finer qualities."

Darcy laughed. "You weren't the only one." She bestowed a warm smile on Prudence.

"That's why I've come here to bring her home." Michael addressed the group, but he looked at Prudence, a hint of appeal in his eyes.

Her heartbeat stuttered. *He still wants to be married.*

"'I will be master of what is mine own,'" Gideon intoned. With a mischievous glance between Michael and Prudence, he settled his warm gaze on his wife and quoted Petruchio. "'She is my goods, my chattels, she is my house, my horse, my ox, my ass, my any thing, and here she stands.'"

Darcy blushed becomingly and glanced self-consciously around the table.

"I've heard of your penchant for quotes," Michael said to Gideon. "I'll fall far behind you on most philosophers and poets and such but *not* on *The Taming of the Shrew*. I once had a schoolteacher who crammed that play down our throats. Made us memorize copious parts." He reached over and took Prudence's hand, giving her fingers a kiss. "'And bonny Pru and sometimes Pru the curst...'" He substituted Kate's name with Prudence's.

"Michael!" Prudence flushed and tried to pull away. *Cursed, indeed.*

Her husband retained possession of her hand. "There is more my dear, but all in praise, I assure you. Shall I go on?"

Suddenly shy at this attention, she nodded.

Michael smiled at everyone, and then only and intimately at her. "'But Pru, the prettiest Pru in Christendom. Pru of Prudence Hall, my super-dainty Pru.'"

Surely Michael doesn't mean that. But she couldn't stop hope from rising at the look of love in his eyes.

"'For dainties are all Pru, and therefore, Pru, Take this of me, Pru of my consolation; Hearing thy mildness praised in every town, Thy virtues spoke of, and thy beauty sounded, Yet not so deeply as to thee belongs, Myself am moved to woo thee for my wife.'"

Darcy and Lina burst out laughing.

Gideon nodded in obvious approval.

Michael raised an eyebrow at the group. "I speak in all seriousness. My wife has won over the people of Morgan's Crossing."

Lina beamed at Prudence. "We heard the story, and Darcy and I are *most* proud." She lifted her water glass. "I think we should have a toast."

Everyone raised their glasses.

Lina's sparkling gaze roved around the table. "To Mail-Order Brides of the West!"

"To Mail-Order Brides of the West," everyone chorused.

Lina swung her glass in Prudence's direction. "To our newest newlyweds, Michael and Prudence."

"To Michael and Prudence!"

A glow from their gleeful attention flooded Prudence's body.

Darcy set down her glass and leaned forward. "But there is one thing Prudence needs from you," she said to Michael, her tone casual, although her eyes gleamed with humor.

"And what is that?" Michael asked.

"A new parasol."

Laughter bubbled up in Prudence, and everyone joined her, even the men. *Michael must have shared the story with Jonah and Gideon.*

Prudence reveled in their expressions of merriment and dared hope she and Michael were forming new friendships.

Michael squeezed her hand. "I already intend to place an order the very next time El Davis arrives in town.

After dinner, hand in hand, Prudence and Michael wandered along a game trail by a meandering stream sheltered by tall trees, talking about their fight. They'd begun with Michael's heartfelt apology for not appreciating her many talents and her attempt to be his helpmate.

His genuine remorse made hope rise in her, but Prudence still couldn't completely banish her doubts. She launched into her concerns about the store and how she'd begun to research possible wrongdoing. She took hope from how carefully he listened, nodding in places and sometimes asking questions.

Michael paused at a grassy bank, sheltered by a line of trees and bushes. He took a deep breath. "After you left, I looked at your calculations and realized Hugely's stealing from me."

"Are you angry with him?"

"Yes. With myself more, though. I should have worked more on them, paid closer attention."

"You have the lives and safety of the miners and their families upon your shoulders, as well as running the mine. That is a heavy burden, Michael," she rested a hand on his forearm. "You can't do everything."

He slanted a roguish glance at her. "Are you interested in the position of bookkeeper?"

"You want me to teach school *and* do your bookkeeping?" she teased. "What's next, running the store?"

"Might be a good idea. I'm in need of a cook and housekeeper, too."

"Humph." She broke their grip and flounced away, tossing a flirtatious look over her shoulder.

"Don't forget someone to warm my bed," Michael teased, catching up with her. He took her hand, and his expression sobered. "I'll hire a schoolmaster for that school you want. He can live in my old cabin. I'll hire a storekeeper, too. But I don't believe anyone could keep my books better than you, my darling Pru." He gazed into her eyes. "Nor keep me warm at night."

Tingles raced through her. Slowly she turned to face him. "From now on, I promise to consider your many worries and keep a more lady-like tone, even when I'm impatient or angry."

He cocked an eyebrow, his eyes glinting. "No more screeching?"

Prudence remembered the tray of biscuits she tossed across the agency kitchen. "Screeching *or* throwing things."

He chuckled. "Throwing things, eh. I think I've had a lucky escape."

She tightened her fingers around his arm. "No escape for you, Mr. Morgan. You are mine."

His expression sobered. "I was wrong. I misjudged you, lost my temper, didn't give you a chance to explain, and drove you off." He swallowed. "You've taught me some mighty hard lessons about my character these last days, Pru. Living hard out here, a man has to be ruthless to succeed in mining, but that attitude doesn't apply to his family. I'm a reformed man. I love you, and I want to work for your love."

He loves me. Prudence pressed a hand to her heart, too moved to speak. She had to catch her breath before she could reply. "You aren't the only one who needed reforming. Michael, most of my life—since I was eight, really, when my sister Lissa died— I've been a dreadful person. The only way I seemed to get any attention from my parents was to have a temper tantrum. I was critical and cruel to everyone. Lina and Darcy have every reason to dislike me, for I was so mean to them. I'm only here at the Barretts' because I had nowhere else to go."

"Perhaps, Darcy and Lina *weren't* your friends. But I can see the bonds of friendship forming between you three."

"I hope you're right."

Michael touched a finger to the tip of her nose. "No *hoping* about it, my dear. I'm your husband. I'm always right." He puffed out his chest, obviously jesting.

Prudence rolled her eyes. "You seemed quite comfortable with Jonah and Gideon."

"Well..." he drawled. "Amazing how swapping stories about mail-order wives creates manly kinship. All we lacked was beer. Remind me to bring a keg when next we visit."

"We'll be visiting?"

"Only if doing so makes you happy."

"I never thought I'd want to visit Lina and Darcy." She shook her head, still shocked by the change in her relationship with the two women. "Trudy, too, for I'll need to make peace with her."

Michael took her hand and drew her closer. "On the drive over here, I promised myself I'd tread carefully regarding an intimate relationship and refrain from touching you." He squeezed her hand. "I've already broken that promise."

"I *suppose* I could forgive you." Prudence peeked at Michael through her lashes and flashed him a coy smile. "I *suppose* I could also love you…and grant you permission to touch my person," she said in mock regal tones.

Eyes twinkling, Michael tapped his mouth. "Come kiss me, my Pru." He misquoted Petruchio and held out his arms.

Laughter bubbled up. "Gladly." She melted into his embrace, tilting her face and pressing her lips to his. The touch of his mouth filled her with a profound sense of wonder, a knowledge that they'd just embarked on a lifetime journey of discovery.

Michael pulled back a few inches and smiled. "That's a promise for the future, wife. And here's another." He lowered his face to kiss her again.

Epilogue

Morgan's Crossing, Montana Territory
September 7th

Dear Bertha,

I'm writing you an apology for how dreadfully I've treated you. Marriage to Mr. Morgan and living in a tiny Western town has opened my eyes to my true character. While I won't go so far as to say I'm reformed—and I've forbidden Michael to use the word tamed—I've become a much better person and am now ashamed of my cruel behavior toward you. I hope the time will come when you'll find it in your generous heart to forgive me.

I'm also writing to you with a job offer. The boarding house in Morgan's Crossing where twenty-five miners live is in need of a cook and housekeeper. I will not spare you the details—the house is a dreadful place—a pigpen where the men are fed slop. I've prevailed upon my husband to hire someone to replace the man who's currently in charge. I'm recommending you with praise for your patient character, your excellent habits in regard to work and cleanliness, and your fine biscuits. (The current proprietor makes ones like stone!)

My husband will pay you a generous salary (I will see to that) but more importantly, you will be needed, and I suspect that fact may be the most enticing to you.

There are few women in this town—ten, counting me. But those few are congenial and have been of great support to me. Perhaps several can spare you a few hours a week to help with housekeeping chores. But there's no available woman to be a full-time maid, although two Oriental boys work at the boarding house and are in need of training. Perhaps you know of a girl or woman who'd be glad to take on the job and move out here with you.

Whatever you decide, I wish you all the best.

Sincerely,

Mrs. Michael Morgan (the former Prudence Crawford)

THE END

A Note to My Readers

Thank you for reading *Mail-Order Brides of the West: Prudence*. When Caroline Fyffe and I planned The Mail-Order Brides of the West Series, we had no thought of Prudence Crawford having her own story. Our idea was for me to write about Trudy, Lina, and Darcy and for Caroline to write about Evie, Heather, and Kathryn. Prudence and Bertha Bucholtz were only meant to be secondary characters. But so many of our readers begged for Prudence and Bertha to have their own stories that we decided I would write them.

Caroline and I designed the bride books to be read in pairs—*Trudy* and *Evie*, *Lina* and *Heather*, and *Darcy* and *Kathryn*. Although readers can go straight through my half of the books, *Trudy, Lina, Darcy*, which take place in the wider world of the Montana Sky Series, or first read *Evie, Heather, Kathryn*, which are set in Caroline's McCutcheon Family Series. (In Kathryn's letter to Darcy, she hints at the events in *Montana Snowfall: McCuthcheon Family Series Book 7.*

Prudence and Bertha's stories will both be set in Morgan's Crossing, as will some future Montana Sky stories. I will have some big surprises for my readers in February 2016, starting with the release of *Mail-Order Brides of the West: Bertha*. Her story will be a *novella*—shorter than the other mail-order bride stories. Be sure you sign up for my newsletter (http://debraholland.com)) for updates.

Next up in the Montana Sky Series is *Healing Montana Sky*, which will be released on October 27th and is currently available for preorder. Look for more exciting Montana Sky stories in Spring 2016.

About

MAIL-ORDER BRIDES OF THE WEST:

Bertha

Bertha Bucholtz returns to her St. Louis home after an unsuccessful stay at the mail-order bridal agency. Her family house is overflowing with her thin, beautiful sisters and their many suitors, and shy, overweight Bertha is lost among the chaos. Even her baking skills—so praised at the agency—aren't special, for her six sisters and her mother are also excellent cooks. Desperate to be living on her own, Bertha searches for a job as a cook but with little success.

Then a letter arrives from her nemesis at the bridal agency. Shrewish Prudence Crawford, now Mrs. Michael Morgan, invites Bertha to move to Morgan's Crossing, Montana Territory and work as a cook and housekeeper at the boarding house for her husband's miners.

Upon her arrival in Morgan's Crossing, Bertha has to contend with Prudence, who seems to have mellowed—or has she? The boarding house is dirty, run-down, and full of uncouth miners. As the only single woman for miles around and a lauded cook, Bertha quickly becomes the siren of the tiny town as well as nearby Sweetwater Springs, as miners and cowboys flock to court her. Now the shy woman who had no choice of suitors has an abundance of them to pick from. She never would have dreamt having too many swains was a bigger problem than having none at all.

February 2, 2016

About

Healing Montana Sky

After a grizzly bear kills Antonia Valleau's trapper husband, she packs her few worldly possessions, leaves her home in the mountains of Montana, and treks to nearby Sweetwater Springs, seeking work to provide for her two young sons.

Reeling from the loss of his wife during childbirth, Erik Muth must find a nursing mother for his newborn daughter to survive. For their children's sake, Erik and Antonia wed, starting a new life together on his farm on the prairie. But it's no easy union. Antonia misunderstands Erik's quiet personality. He finds her independence disconcerting. Both hide secrets that challenge their growing intimacy.

When Indians steal livestock from farms around Sweetwater Springs to feed their starving tribe, the outraged townsfolk demand retaliation. Erik and Antonia must work together to prevent a massacre. Will a marriage forged in loss blossom into love?

October 27, 2015

Montana Sky Series

In chronological order:

1882
Beneath Montana's Sky

1886
Mail-Order Brides of the West: Trudy
Mail-Order Brides of the West: Lina
Mail-Order Brides of the West: Darcy
Mail-Order Brides of the West: Prudence
Mail-Order Brides of the West: Bertha (February 2016)

1890s
Wild Montana Sky
Starry Montana Sky
Stormy Montana Sky
Montana Sky Christmas
A Valentine's Choice
Irish Blessing (March 2016)
Painted Montana Sky
Glorious Montana Sky
Healing Montana Sky
Sweetwater Springs Christmas
Sweetwater Springs Scrooge
Mystic Montana Sky (Summer 2016)

2015
Angel in Paradise

About the Author

Debra Holland is the *New York Times* and *USA Today* Bestselling author of the *Montana Sky Series* (sweet, historical Western romance) and *The Gods' Dream Trilogy* (fantasy romance).

Debra is a three-time Romance Writers of America® Golden Heart® finalist and one-time winner. In 2013, Amazon selected *Starry Montana Sky* as one of the top 50 Greatest Love Stories.

When she's not writing, Dr. Debra works as a psychotherapist and corporate crisis/grief counselor. She's the author of *The Essential Guide to Grief and Grieving*, a book about helping people cope with all kinds of loss. She's also a contributing author to *The Naked Truth About Self-Publishing*.

Debra lives in Southern California with her dog and two cats, who keep her company while she writes. You'll often see pictures of her animals on Debra's social media pages. Sign up for her newsletter and receive a free download of the ebooklet, *58 Tips for Getting What You Want From a Difficult Conversation* at http://drdebraholland.com

You can contact Debra at:
Facebook: https://www.facebook.com/debra.holland.731
Twitter: http://twitter.com/drdebraholland
Blog: http://drdebraholland.blogspot.com

Made in United States
Orlando, FL
24 January 2023

29011117R00136